This Large Print Edition, prepared especially for 2020 Press Home Library, contains the complete unabridged text of the original manuscript.

This is a work of fiction, inspired by actual events. Names, towns, and business establishments are the product of the author's imagination. Any resemblance to persons living or dead is coincidental.

Printed and bound in the United States of America

Published by 2020 PRESS, Tucson, Arizona

ISBN-13: 978-1974682232

LCCN: 2017913413.

2020
PRESS

story consultant: Steve Hameroff
cover art and design: F. Chalmers McGee

Waiting For Friday

Frank McGee

for Helen McGee
gifted co-conspirator
brightened every word and life

Author's note:

The investigation into the 1942 rape and murder of Ursula Ketterman went wrong from the start. The case is still listed as an unsolved homicide in Keaton County, California, where the spectacular court house in Tigh Harbor holds files of the two trials in the case. The first trial, in the summer of 1951, made national news. It garnered columns in *Time*, pages in LIFE, and exhaustive coverage in the Tigh Harbor *Patriot,* the newspaper of J. Kenneth Caulfield, Tigh Harbor's leading citizen. In comparison, the second trial, went almost unnoticed. You might well wonder why.

Decades later, during a dinner party at our house in Newport Beach, California, a neighbor startled all of us with an astonishing story–a lurid tale of sex, rape, medical malpractice, newspaper wars, and murder. Our guest had grown up in Tigh Harbor, knew the secrets and hopes of its residents, and was now a successful Orange County business owner. She insisted that both the legal arguments and the coverage of the case in local and national media had missed the true story, and that everything she told us at the table that night could easily be confirmed.

Easily? This didn't fit at all with Tigh Harbor's tony public image. Why, I asked her, was there never a word about this startling affair in the *Patriot*?

Everyone looked in anticipation at our friend. Her return look was stark. *"Isn't it obvious?"*

In these pages, another publisher, young, determined, impassioned, sets out to learn what really happened to Ursula Ketterman. Sarah Baker had compelling and very personal reasons to pursue the investigation, but little awareness of how hazardous it would become, or how its tentacles might wrap around the unlikely, especially those she loved.

Names have been changed here, and you won't find Tigh Harbor on the map. But you can guess. The picture-perfect city where this story took place exists, right there on the craggy California coast.

PART ONE

(FROM THE RECORD)

LOS ANGELES NEWS COURIER

Special Report: SouthCoast Regional Press

Sunday, August 30, 1942

Shortly after daybreak this morning, the brutalized body of 20 year old Ursula Ketterman, reported missing since Friday, was discovered on a hillside residential property above Feather Rock, a bedroom community adjacent to picturesque Tigh Harbor. Keaton County Sheriff J. Edmond Russell called the crime "unimaginable."

June, 1956

As cemeteries go, this one boasted a view, a benefit lost on the 436 souls for whom this favored bit of California real estate was the final resting place.

Sarah Baker pondered the irony and slowed her Plymouth to a stop as the headstones came into sight. To the southwest, the tile-roofed homes and businesses of Tigh Harbor strung themselves elegantly along the crescent of the bay, a terra cotta shawl around the shoulders of the city. She eased her foot off the brake and let the car roll to the cemetery entrance. Then she turned off the key, and shivered. The Ketterman girl had been murdered close by. Sarah's own brush with death had happened right here.

Damn, that was years ago.

She stepped out and faced the gates. At midday on a Monday, she was at a place she had hated to remember, but couldn't forget. She needed to come here today. But in the movie of her mind she was suddenly back a decade, running for her life.

In 1946 she'd been a freshman at Tigh Harbor Junior College, following the grueling training regime that had made her a high school track star. When her afternoon chemistry classes at the JC finished for the day she would often don gym shorts and a sleeveless blouse, tie her wavy auburn hair into a pony tail, and head up this road toward the highlands, to increase her stamina and stretch long legs that loved to run. That day would be her last workout before the final meet of the year.

Two miles above the city just past the cemetery she heard a vehicle laboring up the hill. Minutes later a dirty brown International pickup truck with a defective muffler flew by her, and she glimpsed its driver, tossing his head from side to side to the blaring beat of a radio. Seconds later he stopped his truck with a screech, spun the vehicle around, and headed back toward her. She slowed to a walk. The radio vied with the racket of the exhaust. He steered onto the shoulder, aimed the vehicle directly at her, and stopped. Fear hit her like a hammer. She saw him smirk through the grimy glass, still rocking his head to the murderous metronome of the beat. Then he turned off the ignition and the silence was terrifying.

She spun around and ran toward the city. The machine roared to life, and with tires spitting gravel it raced directly toward her. Wheeling to the right, Sarah vaulted the wall of the cemetery. The truck slid to a stop and the driver leapt out and came after her on foot. She flew among the gravestones, leapt across a freshly dug grave, and nearly fell on the piled up dirt beyond. Her mind raced, her feet raced, and her pursuer raced. Pumped by an unknown something he gained on her. Panic and fear failed to give her wings. Then a slim chance of escape flashed into her mind.

A family plot with a wrought iron fence around it was just ahead of her. She darted behind the barrier, stopped, and turned to face her attacker. For seconds they were frozen, she with her heart pounding in her chest, he taunting her across the fence. Then she feinted to the left, and when he lurched that way she reversed to the right, and with an explosion of speed headed back toward the dirt pile. She went over the top and down the other side, leaping across the open grave. He was not so fortunate. Racing to the top, he jumped through the air and landed at the bottom of the grave, screaming with rage. Sarah sprinted to the truck, grabbed the keys from the ignition and threw them far into the bushes. Trembling, she ran for the city, for the campus, for the dorm, for safety.

Two hours later, with the campus security officer and her roommate, she was back at the site. They found no vehicle. Just skid marks, and gouges where the attacker had climbed out of the grave.

A burly sheriff arrived and Sarah told him all she could remember about the driver.

"He must have hot-wired his pickup," the sheriff said. "It has at least a hundred twins around here. We'll file a report, but finding him is a long shot." The security officer told the girls to get in his car for the return to the campus. Sarah looked back, saw the sheriff standing with crossed arms by his patrol cruiser, his face as angry as a thunder cloud. It struck her as odd, but only briefly. *We're close to where the Ketterman girl was killed.*

She knew it was irrational, but didn't call her father to tell him what happened until late that night. He was shaken, and so was she. She hated not being in control of things. After all, she was going-on nineteen.

At the track meet on Saturday, to the fist pumps of her father and the cheers of the crowd in the stands, Sarah won the last race of the day, the 800 meters, pulling away from the field. Afterwards she said to her coach, "I didn't know until two days ago how fast I could be."

"What happened two days ago?" he asked.

"I raced a devil in a graveyard."

The coach looked blank, then smiled. *Just a young girl's figure of speech*. On graduation day, fifteen days after the cemetery escape, she announced to her father that she wanted to enroll at U.C. Berkeley.

* * * *

Sarah Baker shook her head, took a breath, and closed the car door. She wasn't just a terrified JC freshman running away from a crazy person in a graveyard now. She'd finished university, worked for two years in Europe with the Marshall Plan, snagged a lucrative job with a big company in the Pacific Northwest, taken over *The Echo*, her father's newspaper, and begun probing a scandal that might implicate the son of a leading citizen.

But 24 hours ago she'd had an ugly blowup with Martin, her husband of less than a year.

Just your typical Saturday, Sare.

Tomorrow, in Los Angeles, Sarah was placing all her

eggs in a single basket. If they didn't break, *The Echo* could double it's reach, be more profitable, and she could savor revenge on her father's nemesis, that ugly "leading citizen," who had lived in this beautiful place.

According to a telephoned tip from Kathy Stroud, her university roommate, a lead in Sarah's potentially sensational investigation was lying six feet under, somewhere inside this cemetery gate. She moved carefully through the entrance, stepped onto the grass, and for a crazy moment wondered if anyone ever practiced putting here.

She walked toward the ocean, along the headstones, past family plots, and there saw names she recognized, families of childhood friends. At the very edge of the cemetery she found the Caulfield site. Kenneth Caulfield's monument dominated it.

His parents were at his left, both his wives at his right. Next to them there was space for his older son, and for his daughters and their spouses. Then, just as Kathy Stroud had promised, she found the marker, a plain stone on the newest grave, the grass trimmed flush with its polished grey surface. It read:

Timothy Caulfield, 1923 – 1955.

Well damn! Timmy, Kathy was right. You didn't just drop off the planet after all. Where have you been? Dad knew you were out there somewhere. Did your father push the silver spoon too far down your throat? Will you tell us why that girl was killed? And who did it?

Timmy's grave was just a year old, so where and how he died should not be hard to discover. But there was a great deal to think about, and do. Sarah turned from the Caulfield site and walked back to her car, her thoughts a maelstrom.

The flight wasn't until 4:30, and there was plenty of time to get to the airport. But Sarah was uneasy. She was about to take a big financial leap.

Without Ernie I wouldn't even have considered it.

She drove on down the hill into town. Traffic was light and the afternoon beautiful, but thoughts kept jumping through her mind like kangaroos.

Lord, what a scene yesterday. What was Martin thinking? Is he really that cynical? About the paper? About Oak Hills? About me? He's been distant lately, and often sarcastic, but I never expected an insult like that: "Fucking Ernie!" Damn it, no! Ernie is a terrific journalist and my major ally at the paper. And that's all.

Ten minutes later she realized she'd been driving with no clear destination. She had turned onto Cypress, and there, at the end of the cul-de-sac, was the house she'd grown up in, looking pretty much as she remembered it. The trees at the back were taller, reaching above the second story, and the bushes in front were different. But the paint looked the same, and a family with children must live there. A small red Radio wagon was in the driveway and a dinged up Schwinn bike lay on the grass. Maybe its owner rode it home from school like her brother.

Georgie would race down the street, hit the lawn, slam on his brakes, and end up facing the other way. Daddy was never home to catch him at it, but he knew why the grass wouldn't grow on that side of the yard. When Georgie first got the bike, he'd skid his tire on the sidewalk, compete with his buddies to make the longest mark; 'Lay a strip' they'd called it. Then when Daddy told him he'd have to buy his own tires, he'd switched his acrobatics to the lawn.

The living room was on the left, the dining room on the right. It was just behind those windows, she remembered, at the supper table in 1939, that her father made her aware of just how radioactive the Caulfield name could be.

* * * *

That meal began as just another family dinner. Sarah, 12 but very much going-on 13, had been at this table with these same people for most of the meals she had ever eaten. Her father sat at the head, her mother at the foot, Georgie by the kitchen, Sarah by the window. The oilcloth table cover showed wear, but the green and white checkerboards made it easy to align the silverware.

"Daddy, Patsy and I had our tennis lesson this afternoon, and do you know they play tennis on grass in England? How can they do that? Wouldn't they slip all the time? How could the ball bounce? What if it rains and everything stays wet? Why don't they play on cement like everybody else?"

Her brother shook his head. "Hey, why don't you just ask your coach or read a book? Do we have to answer a hundred stupid questions every time you hear something new?"

Louise Baker looked at her children with an air of pleasant resignation. Both were bright, both ambitious, and though their interests frequently went in opposite directions, she felt their relationship, and the mostly benign bickering that marked it, was healthy, even if Georgie's language was sometimes tasteless.

"Questions aren't automatically stupid, Georgie, dear. Only stupid questions are stupid. Like, 'Why do I have to brush my teeth?'" She looked knowingly at her son, but her eyes gave her away. They both began to laugh and Sarah, in spite of herself, joined in.

"Okay, Mom, but I was only five," Georgie protested. "I think that was a pretty logical question for five."

Dinner conversations at the Baker home were lively, and bad moods not entertained. If one of the family had a problem or was unhappy, by the time the pie or rice pudding was served, the mood had generally changed. Louise was the catalyst. Her husband provided a good home for them all, and she knew he loved each one passionately, albeit quietly. In recent months he seemed to make less effort to participate in family conversations, although he was always the most knowledgeable. But since her illness had been diagnosed and begun to manifest itself, his lightness of spirit had gradually lessened, and while Louise would never have described him as temperamental, it was poignant to her how much he had changed.

She could not fault him for this, nor did she spend a moment berating herself. In spite of her Presbyterian upbringing, she had enough true faith to know that there was no guilt ordained along with her multiple sclerosis, only the commission, and the privilege, of using every beat of her heart to bring joy to her family.

* * * *

Baker's was Tigh Harbor's second newspaper. He had launched it in 1923, two years after he married Louise, and two years before Georgie was born. It was a feisty paper, frequently contrarian, and invariably at odds with the editorial policies of Kenneth Caulfield's *Patriot,* which had begun publishing in 1910. The ongoing debates between the papers were a topic of daily conversation in the city. Tourists and part-timers missed much of the drama, but the natives did not; no love was lost between George Baker and Kenneth Caulfield.

Until this evening, Baker's children might as well have been tourists. They had no idea of his struggles, nor the potential implications for themselves.

George Jr. turned toward his father. "Dad, the troop is going up to the Junipero Serra campsite during Easter break for a merit badge campout. My sleeping bag is hardly even a rag anymore, and I really need one with a nylon cover. It's gonna be cold up there, too. Could I get a new one at Weil's this week? Timmy's dad got him one and he says it's as warm as toast. And did you know Mr. Caulfield is renting a bus for us? He even says he'll run a picture in his paper of all of us climbing on board. Isn't that keen?"

Baker suddenly banged his fork down on his plate so loudly that Sarah thought he might have cracked it. "Keen? Keen? Did you say keen? Dammit, man, that's not 'keen'! That's just another yellow ad for the omnipotence of the *Patriot,* and the Scouts are happy to go along with it."

Everyone stopped eating.

"Well, of course you want the bus. But do you think Caulfield is getting you the bus just to take you up to the mountain? Not on your life. He's paying 50 bucks for the bus, and for his goddam charity he's getting 500 dollars worth of publicity."

Nobody around the table moved. Sarah had heard her father swear, but never at the table, and never in front of anyone in the family. Finally her mother said, "Yes, George, I guess he'll be getting his money's worth."

After nearly a minute of looking down at the remains

of his string beans and pot roast, Baker said quietly, "I apologize to you all for that." He looked in turn at each of them, starting with Louise, and Sarah was aware of something in his face she had never seen before, a grudging admission that he was not Superman after all. Like many 12-year-old daughters of strong fathers, Sarah had all her life been secure in her father's infallibility. This was the first suggestion she had ever seen of his not being in control. She was startled by it, and puzzled. She couldn't understand what it meant.

"Mother," Baker said, "if we could have some of that pie I was smelling when I came home, there's some things I'd like to tell you all."

Sarah knew her parents were linked at the heart, and her self confidence reflected the closeness of the family. Louise knew a great deal about the workings of her husband's newspaper, and often gave him insights about the community, and occasionally business ideas. But there was a level he had protected the family from, and tonight, after the outburst that was like a pressure cooker valve release for him, he decided to include everyone in what was really happening.

Calling his troops to attention was not Baker's typical style. Sarah and Georgie looked intently toward their father. "Your mother and I have been talking for months about changes that may be ahead of us," he began, as Louise walked slowly into the kitchen. "I've told you before about our battle for advertising revenue. That's really where we make our money. The *Sentinel* is the best paper in town, and there's been no question about that for 17 years. But today we're facing crooked competition. Beginning just over a year ago Kenneth Caulfield began cheating the public.

"It's called yellow journalism. He's blurred the line so slickly between editorial and advertising that you can't trust any of his coverage today. People are reading PR releases instead of news stories and don't even know it. It's in lots of the *Patriot's* copy. Of course his advertisers are delighted. They say, 'Look at what the *Patriot* wrote about our company, Baker!' 'We're getting a lot more for our money from the *Patriot,* Baker!' We're being deserted right and left by people we've always produced business for. And Carlson and all his law partners agree that our hands are tied, legally at least."

"What's that mean, Dad?"

"Son, it means that unless we can find a way to increase our revenue, we may have to close the shop. If we'd stoop to swim in the sewer with Caulfield we'd probably flourish. But I'd rather sleep at night than sell my independence. Caulfield put two other papers out of business before you kids were born. Now he wants to buy us out, and I shudder to think what he'd do with the *Sentinel*. I'm not about to give him the opportunity, even if folding the paper is the only way to stop him."

"Daddy!"

"Jeeze, Pop, all because of advertising?"

"Yes, all because of that. If we didn't carry advertising we'd have to charge double or triple for subscriptions, and the public just wouldn't understand why. Anyway, people want to read ads almost as much as the news. Caulfield has been playing this game ever since we seriously started cutting into his circulation. He picked off nearly a hundred of our subscribers. Now he's bought off most of the advertisers in town. The guy's a whore."

"George, that's just not table talk," scolded Louise, bringing a still warm berry pie from the kitchen to place in front of her husband. "You just slice up this pie and pretend it's Caulfield. Try a little voodoo on him. He's a rotten man, I know, but this is dinner." She stood behind him and gently placed her hands on the sides of his head, hands that now had lost almost all sensation. She leaned forward and kissed him on the forehead.

Baker showed a suggestion of a smile, turned to look into the eyes of his partner of 19 years. "Mother, what an amazing woman you are. Voodoo is the obvious answer. Of course plenty of people have asked why I don't just expose him, but I don't see any way to win in that. We'd be back on the grade school playground. 'Teacher, Kennie doesn't play fair.' 'Teacher, Kennie stole my lollipop.' Besides, we'd also be accusing most of the businesses in town of trying to put something over on the public."

He handed Louise her slice of pie, passed one to Sarah and an extra large serving to George, Jr. "Kids, here's what we're going to do . . ."

The family would move to Oak Hills, a town of about 3,000, 75 miles inland, and Baker would launch a weekly there. Oak Hills had not had a newspaper for a decade, since Able Weisenthal died at age 94. Forty-eight years earlier, Able, who owned Oak Hills' only dry goods store, had begun producing a one-page monthly announcement of births, weddings and local goings on. It was good for business, he said, and gave him something to do when he had no customers, which in those days happened a lot. Sixty seven families lived in the town at the time. Several wars later *The Echo* still echoed, then an eight page fortnightly that Baker's *Sentinel* printed in Tigh Harbor under contract, because Able never bought a printing press. Everybody in Oak Hills read *The Echo* then. Now Baker would pick up the name for his new paper, and he knew that most families in town would become subscribers.

PART TWO

Sarah drove into Tigh Harbor's picturesque airport and parked, her body at the wheel, her mind still back in the eighth grade. The lot was only half full. She could have driven to L.A. in less than four hours, but today she had opted to fly. The terminal was typical Tigh Harbor architecture, with terra cotta roofs and arched Spanish entryways. She checked in at the counter, and with her small Grasshopper bag in hand, walked along the polished tiles, turned right and stepped out onto the tarmac.

It had been two years since the plane from Seattle had brought her here, when she had given up her marketing career to become publisher of *The Echo,* ninety minutes up the mountain in Oak Hills. Adventurous years. Scary, exciting, romantic, fulfilling years; and looking back at this particular moment, a crazy mix of promise and disillusion.

Two ground crew members were pushing a cart of luggage toward the aircraft, a British made turbo prop with its own entry system; stairs folded into the rear of the plane like a double-jointed blade on a jackknife. As the plane gained altitude and turned south, she settled into her seat and looked back at the road leading up the ridge, past the houses on the hill and the cemetery at the top. She remembered the first time she'd traveled up that road, when the family moved to Oak Hills. *I think I must have cried the whole way . . .*

This morning she had seen the polished stone on the grave of Timothy Caulfield. Now *The Echo* had it's first lead toward answering the sixty-four dollar question: Who killed Ursula Ketterman? The courts had provided no answer. Ursula was murdered fourteen years ago, violated and brutalized. There were trials in 1951 and 1952. The man who was charged went free. The killer could be living in a house she could see below her right now.

Thirty minutes later, a smartly dressed stewardess walked down the aisle to make sure everyone was strapped in for landing. Sarah tightened her seat belt. The plane touched down, taxied to the gate, and the stair in the tail was lowered. She lifted her bag from the rack and headed for the terminal. In terms of hubbub, Los Angeles and Tigh Harbor were at opposite ends of the scale. Sarah was ever aware of how different the pace of life had been for her since she'd moved to Oak Hills, which was even more mellow than Tigh Harbor. For a moment, the commotion of L.A. assailed her, and the unnatural air.

Then she was quickly back in the role of professional woman. She was a publisher now. She'd been a sales and marketing specialist, traveled all over the Western States, and before that worked in Paris with the Marshall Plan.

Yet she remembered feeling this way when she'd come home from Europe, back to a different world. Twenty-four months on a continent digging out from the ugly rubble of war had given her a view of life she'd not imagined before. She had worked mostly with Americans in Europe, in an over-crowded requisitioned office in Paris, a treeless island surrounded by seas of lost loved ones, lost homes and hopes.

The Marshall Plan was a lifeboat for the continent. At first she'd paid attention, and allowed the daily dramas of families struggling to recover from devastation to play out on the stages of her mind. But after a year, when her emotions began to speak too loudly, she had sloughed off any pretension of being a secular savior, and immersed herself in the work.

But she remembered arriving in New York back then on the venerable S.S. America, stepping out into the city, and being startled by the abundance. No one seemed to lack for anything–food, cars, clothing, or pleasures.

At the taxi ramp outside the LAX terminal Sarah got into a Yellow Cab and told the driver to take her to the Century Hotel on Santa Monica Boulevard. It wouldn't be elegant, Mrs. Cardenas had warned, but was within walking distance of her appointment in the morning. After check-in she smiled at the venerable bellhop, said "No thanks, it's really light," and carried her bag to the elevator. The floor indicator above the door swung back to one, and there was an attendant at the control. Her room was on the third floor. Not exactly a big publisher's suite, she mused, but I'm not exactly a big publisher. Yet. She grinned at the thought, performed her ablutions, and went back down to the lobby.

She wondered how long this old hotel would continue to exist in this rapidly changing part of town. It was as time-worn as the bellhop. The back lot of 20th Century Fox Studios was right next door. It had once been the Tom Mix Ranch, owned by a movie cowboy of her childhood. How times change. Across the street the quaint yellow sign of a restaurant invited her to a Mexican dinner, and she decided to accept. *Las Casitas* had once been two homes, nicely spliced together into an attractive restaurant years before. California had once been Spanish-speaking country. She'd always loved Mexican food, but never had a Mexican friend until moving to Oak Hills. That move had changed her life in every aspect, she mused, pulling open the restaurant door. She was warmly welcomed, shown to a table, and ordered Chile Rellenos. Would they be as good as those made by Elena's mother?

* * * *

Elena Cardenas had become Sarah's best friend within days of the Baker family's arrival in Oak Hills. A lively, popular, Tigh Harbor 12-year old, Sarah had felt pummeled by the events preceding the "move," which she disdained as a despicable four-letter-word. The last undimmed celebration of 1940 in the family's Tigh Harbor Cypress Street home was a Sunday dinner on August

25 to celebrate Georgie's 15th birthday.

Five weeks later, at the end of September, her father announced that the move to Oak Hills was scheduled for late November. He affirmed that it was a challenging time to be changing towns, businesses, homes and schools, but made clear that it was dictated by economics. Sarah would be in the middle of the eighth grade. In Oak Hills, 450 junior high and high school students took classes in the same building, Oak Hills High School, half of them drawn from the families who owned or worked on the truck farms and ranches surrounding the town. "This is going to be a big change for all of us," Baker told his children, "but I think you're going to like Oak Hills. It will be a wonderful place to live. The drier environment will be better for your mother, and I've found a house without any stairs." He made no reference to relocating away from the toxic business climate in which the affairs of J. Kenneth Caulfield seemed to thrive.

Friends were Sarah's life, and leaving them made the prospect of the move traumatic. The thought of not living forever in Tigh Harbor had never entered her mind before this. And even when she would go away to college, she'd surely come home to Tigh Harbor for Christmas and summer vacations.

On November 22, one day after a surreal Thanksgiving observance with their friends the Temple family, and just six months after her father's momentous announcement at that same table, Baker piled his family into the Buick, their laps loaded to their noses with things that hadn't gone into the moving van, and pointed the car up the Ridge Road. A bevy of Sarah's classmates had come to see them off, and oceans of teenage tears were shed.

No one needed to say good-bye to Georgie. Baker would bring him back to Tigh Harbor and deliver him to the Temples' house Sunday afternoon. He'd be at school on Monday without missing a class, and live with the Temples until Senior graduation. There would be final details on the sale of the office building to take care of on Monday, then Baker would return to Oak Hills. The press and production equipment had already been shipped up the mountain, cement poured for the press foundation, and newsprint and ink orders placed. Baker prepared carefully for everything he did. By now, he knew the road to Oak Hills by heart.

On the hill above town, Sarah pleaded for one last good-bye. "I'll never see my friends again," she wailed. Her father stopped on the roadside above the cemetery, and all four stood looking back over the city. After a moment, Sarah turned and sobbed into her mother's arms, lamenting this unjust violation of her happiness.

Louise Baker had prepared a picnic lunch for the two hour trip. Fifteen minutes after Tigh Harbor was out of sight, Sarah started munching on a jack cheese sandwich with lettuce, mustard and mayo, and Georgie, his sandwich already downed, was drinking a quart of milk. Most of the trip passed with Sarah asking about their new house and school and did they have a good movie theater? They had just gone through a ten-mile stretch of small farms, with rolling fields and alfalfa green from the autumn rains, when they saw the Welcome To Oak Hills sign. Sarah squealed with excitement, "Look Daddy, we're here!" Baker looked over at Louise and both quietly smiled.

Their new house was on the east edge of town, if the town had an edge, which it didn't. Fanning out from the town "center," properties just got a little more rural, eventually becoming small farms. The Bakers' new home was near the end of the transition. It was a ranch-style structure with vertical redwood siding about 18 inches wide, stained a warm brown, the windows outlined with white sills and frames. Built in the 1920s, the house overlooked farmland. The field to the west was a commercial truck garden, with brown-black soil, the kind that would erupt in green within a week of planting. The country road to the town passed to the southwest some fifty feet lower than the house.

The lane onto the property led around the back of the building to the front, which faced east. A porch without a railing ran along the front of the home from end to end, an easy step above a yard of hard packed earth large enough for a basketball game, a tennis court, or a church social on a sunny day. Worn off tufts of grass showed green where water had managed to feed the roots, and cars or farm equipment had given them a chance.

At the north end, three ancient cottonwoods towered above a score of surrounding oaks, shimmering their leaves in welcome to the newcomers in the Buick. A red barn stood at the south end of the yard. The fifty-year-old structure was leased to Henry Shannon, the dairy farmer who owned the adjacent property. He stored hay in the loft there and kept a bull and a few dry guernsey cows. His border collie, Dixie, trotted out of the barn to investigate the visitors, and instantly was adopted by Sarah, which George and Louise had expected. She fell in love with the place the first day.

The house was welcoming. Between two large windows on the west side of the living room a fieldstone fireplace rose to the ceiling, which was paneled with knotty pine. The ceiling was several shades darker around the fireplace now than originally, thanks to twenty years of a hearth that took several minutes to draw. Louise, always aiming for an immaculate home, would come to regard her two-tone ceiling as one of the charms of living in Oak Hills. Sarah never noticed it.

The following Wednesday, Sarah sat beside her father as he drove her to Oak Hills High. Her mother would typically have taken care of things like that, and liked being behind the wheel. But during the preceding six weeks she had fallen several times without warning, and now left the chauffeuring to her husband and son. She used a cane to steady herself when she was on her feet, if no wall or other support was within reach. Otherwise she never gave any reference to being incapacitated. As a result, those she was with usually seemed oblivious of it.

Sarah walked into the school both nervous and excited. The structure was slightly smaller, but with similar red brick architecture, than the Junior High she'd been attending in Tigh Harbor. In her homeroom, the teacher introduced her to the class. When she mentioned that Sarah's family had moved to Oak Hills so her father could start a newspaper, a bloom of enthusiasm erupted over the eighth graders; "comics" and "funny papers" seemed of special interest, Baker noted. He took Sarah to the Rexall Drug Store for ice cream cones before heading home.

At 7:15 the next morning, a pumpkin colored Chevrolet school bus picked up Sarah and three others at the bottom of the lane. One of the three was in her class, two were younger. Her classmate was Elena Cardenas. As the bus bounced along, Sarah discovered that Elena's grandfather, "Papa Beto," owned the field below the Baker's living room window.

On the afternoon ride home Sarah began lamenting to Elena about the friends she had "loved and lost" in Tigh Harbor, including the gorgeous Ricky Scott. Elena made a sorrowful face. Sarah smiled in spite of herself, and they both got the giggles. It was an instant friendship. By the end of the school year they were inseparable. On long summer afternoons, Louise Baker began setting an extra place for supper. Elena's mother, Alexandria, did the same. Blue, farmer Shannon's second dog, was a highly social Australian herder, and often trotted back and forth with the girls as they moved between their houses.

The first time Sarah had gone to the Cardenas home she was surprised to find that Elena and her mother spoke to each other in Spanish. "How come?" she asked.

"Our family came from Mexico," Mrs. Cardenas said, "and everybody speaks Spanish there."

"There are lots of Mexicans in Tigh Harbor," Sarah said, "but I never got to know any."

Alexandria was kneading bread dough at the time, and just for a moment, her hands stopped moving. Then she glanced at her daughter's young guest and smiled.

Sarah failed to note the irony of the exchange, or of the image as she turned at the bottom of the drive to wave good-bye to her friend, who was standing on the porch of the nicest home in the area.

During that first summer the commuting time between the houses got shorter and shorter, as Sarah discovered how much she loved to run. She started timing herself, running against her personal best like an Olympic competitor, pushing her long slim legs a little bit more every day. By the end of the summer she was an athlete. When school began in September, she was the fastest girl in her class. Elena ran back and forth with her between houses but didn't race, because however hard she tried, she couldn't win. Blue always won.

"But that's not a fair race, is it Elena?" Sarah complained one day. "Anyway, he's got two extra legs. and he never even works up a sweat."

"Ha, you just can't bear to lose even to a dog, is that it?"

Elena's family owned one of the three grocery stores in town, the only one that carried the traditional Mexican foods enjoyed by the field workers around Oak Hills. Grandpa Beto had migrated to the U.S. from Saltillo, Mexico, in 1890. For 50 years he had raised vegetables on the 40 lush acres that carpeted the landscape below the Bakers' windows. He had leased the land for a decade, and bought it in 1910, after proving to the local bank that he was a worthy candidate for a mortgage loan. Had he not been so independent, he could have easily obtained money from his family in Mexico to buy the property for cash, but he wanted to build a life of his own. The property owed its year-round productivity to an abundance of water from a spring at its southern edge, water with a mineral content that produced greener and healthier vegetables than those grown in the San Joaquin Valley. A small bottling company used the same spring.

On Friday, January 29, 1941, 64 days after moving his family to Oak Hills, George Baker had produced the first issue of *The Echo,* complete with a front page tribute to "My friend, Able Weisenthal." Every home in town got a complementary copy, and the paper was off and running.

* * * *

31

The Echo's announced editorial focus was on local news, but every week there was a front page story about the war in Europe. Sarah was extremely proud of her father's achievement, and read each article. She did this until Easter, when at the dinner table, Baker said grace before the meal. At occasions like this, such a grace was typically ceremonial, more likely than not the result of a suggestion from her mother.

Baker was undemonstrative, taciturn even, about his religious beliefs. Yet after he had given thanks for the meal that day he prayed that God would receive those who had been lost in the fire bombing of London, and that those who survived would find food and shelter, and be able to maintain their hope. He said Amen, and it was a long moment before anyone, even Georgie, reached for one of the serving bowls heaped with the food that was filling the room with aromas.

During the dinner Sarah joined in the festive conversation, but couldn't stop thinking of her father's prayer. By the time the meal was over, she realized that she had been reading those awful stories of war as if she were reading an English assignment or a comic book. Images streamed through her mind, of pictures she had looked at but not seen, words she'd read but hadn't heard. There had been photos of burning buildings, of ambulance crews, and of subway stations sheltering tens of thousands of Londoners as bombs rained down overhead. There were stories of bravery, suffering, and loss. She was thirteen now, and suddenly she determined not to be just a child anymore. She made a grown up choice: from this moment on she would pay attention.

In the months that followed, Sarah's help was increasingly needed at home. Her mother wore full length dresses, and Sarah understood that the style made her feel more steady on her feet, a little less vulnerable to legs that sometimes failed to support. Louis Baker was tall, equal in height to her husband, more than his equal in inner strength, George Baker commented to Sarah one Sunday evening when the two were reading after dinner. The remark was her father's invitation to share in the part of his life he rarely spoke about. They talked at length.

Baker reminisced how, in his teens, he had been drawn to her mother's beauty, her wavy brown hair and disarming smile, her humor and intelligence, and to some inner quality that was magnetic. As their lives had progressed, he added strength to the list. Now, in her illness, her strength seemed to be what held everything in their world together. He didn't really know where the strength came from, only that he depended on it, on her, and that every moment for the rest of their lives was a moment to cherish. He reviled himself sometimes, he said, at how long it had taken him to become aware of this.

By the middle of Sarah's next school year, Louise Baker had fallen so often she was forced to either stay in bed, remain seated, or use a wheelchair. On weekends, George, Jr., when he wasn't in a football game or practicing, drove his Model A from Tigh Harbor to Oak Hills to help around the house. He moved home for the summer after the father of his girlfriend packed the family off to San Luis Obispo, where he'd been hired to head the city's planning department. Georgie got a summer job in the Cardenas grocery store, then moved back to live in Tigh Harbor with the Temple family for his senior year.

In early December, one day before the Japanese attack on Pearl Harbor, Louise contracted pneumonia in both lungs. Nurses were hired to be in attendance round the clock. A tube from an oxygen tank by her bed allowed her to breath well enough during the next weeks to participate in holiday celebrations with her family, who shared presents, sang carols, and recalled stories about moments in their lives, silly, serious or simply precious. The day after Christmas Georgie left with three of his high school buddies, including Billy Temple, for a week's skiing at Mammoth Mountain. All four planned to enlist in the Navy after they graduated in June. They returned from their ski trip on New Year's Day. Sarah was fourteen.

Her first day back at school was the third of January. After the bus ride home she said good-bye to Elena at the road and walked up the lane to the house. When she turned the corner into the yard she saw oxygen tanks, all four of them, lined up precisely on the porch. Without being aware of it she dropped her books to the ground and stood still. Her eyes filled with tears as she realized her mother wouldn't need the oxygen any more, that she could breathe easily now.

Then came a wondrous sensation, warm, like the warm she used to feel when her mother would tuck her in bed, tell her stories, lay her cheek against her own and kiss her goodnight. Now she could do it again.

Later her father put his arms around her, and she tried to be brave, to think about him, not only of her own sense of loss. But she didn't succeed very well. She knew there was an empty place in her father's heart now that she couldn't fill, couldn't fix. Only fill the empty place she sensed inside herself. She could fix that, and would. That evening she went running until dark. The harder she ran, the less she hurt. When she returned to the house, to her surprise her brother hugged her, held her hands, looked into her eyes. He never did that. It's as hard for him as for me, she thought. During the funeral service he put his arm around her shoulder. The next day Georgie went back to Tigh Harbor, to resume his senior year.

In the weeks that followed, Baker, heartbroken by the loss of his soulmate, comforted Sarah as best he could in a house that now seemed hollow. Sarah was just as eager to comfort him. From the Cardenas family, who virtually adopted them, understanding flowed like a river.

During the rest of that year Sarah walked frequently to her father's office after class. He always welcomed her, and encouraged her obvious interest in advertising and marketing, the commercial side of the paper. As weekly editions of *The Echo* were being prepared, she would pore over ads like a critic, peppering him with questions.

"Dad, the Goodyear ad looks better than Frank's Brakes and Tires. Why doesn't Frank's have a picture? It doesn't get your attention." "Dad, shouldn't Woolworth's say more than '*five-and-ten*?' How about 'More for your Money' or something?" "Dad, Weil's Department Store is always having a sale. If they have sales all the time, won't people just wait till they want something and know there'll always be a sale?" It was clear to Baker that his daughter had a future in advertising or public relations if she wanted it.

Weekends were best. Sometimes Baker would take Sarah and Elena in the Buick, driving to Pismo Beach, or into the Los Padres National Forest, or even as far north as Carmel and Monterey. The girls would play games, make up stories, read the Burma Shave signs nailed onto fence posts along the roads. They talked about their dreams. Elena wanted to be a doctor. Sarah wanted to be like her father. On back roads during those trips Sarah learned to drive. Occasionally they would get rooms in an inexpensive motel, see a movie on Saturday night, breakfast at a coffee shop and be home by Sunday afternoon. Sarah knew she would remember these moments for the rest of her life, heart times with people she loved.

* * * *

Las Casitas had delivered. The meal was fine, the ambience warm, and Sarah had luxuriated in the memories triggered by the experience.

She stepped onto the sidewalk, startled to find that a dry Santa Ana was blowing. The offshore wind had come up suddenly during her visit to the restaurant. The hot blast whipped her hair, peppered her face with dust, pushed her dress against her body like a second skin. The wind shook signs, blew debris, bent trees. It was after nine o'clock but there was still a red-orange glow in the western sky, the color obviously overdone by some amateur celestial artist. She crossed the boulevard, entered the hotel and went up to her room. Wind howled outside and the weathered old windows provided little protection from the noise. But it was not a cold night.

The Santa Ana could blow itself out tonight or continue. California's chameleon character always fascinated, despite the risks that came along with it. A few days of this kind of wind from the desert could parch trees and grasses to tinder, and fires could, and did, flare up, often out of nowhere. Oak Hills was in dry country, but so much farming surrounded the town that irrigation and a few well-placed firebreaks kept the community protected.

Up on the highlands, though, there had been infernos. Smoke would stretch two hundred miles out into the ocean, until the wind changed, and brought moist air back to the coastline, and then, mercifully, to the highlands. Ten years ago, just after her high school graduation, and just before a Santa Ana like the one tonight, there had been no mercy. A night Sarah would never forget.

* * * *

On a late Wednesday afternoon in June, 1945, a school bus accident killed three Oak Hills children and injured nine others, all pre-teens. The town was in shock. Sarah's father knew most of the families, and wept more than once as he worked through Thursday night to prepare coverage of the catastrophe. He wrote not only of the accident, but of the families and the children, careful to reject any photo that would exploit the horror of the scene.

The bus had been taking children to their homes and farms on the western edges of the school district. A semi truck was coming toward the town on the two lane road, laden with farm equipment for the highlands. A light rain had fallen. Suddenly a fawn dashed across the road in front of the truck, closely pursued by a coyote, which in turn was pursued by the doe. The startled driver braked sharply and the truck jackknifed, throwing the densely packed trailer across the oncoming lane directly into the path of the bus. Its driver, who was also the girls' basketball coach, was airlifted along with two children to Tigh Harbor General. Ambulances took the other injured to Mercy Hospital in Oak Hills.

At about 1:00 a.m. Sarah had gone to sleep in the room above her father's office. The narrow stairway was just to the right of the entrance, covered with a threadbare runner that Sarah's mother had asserted was installed a century ago. The tiny apartment had a single bed, a small bathroom and little else. Sarah was wakened by the late May sunrise. During the night the weather had changed and a Santa Ana was blowing. She went downstairs just as her father handed the final copy and photos to the waiting production crew, who immediately went to work on it. Baker leaned back in his old oak swivel chair and rubbed his eyes, red from fatigue. Sarah came behind him and took his head in her hands.

"You're my hero, Daddy."

He put his hands on hers, and for a moment, wept again.

"How about a little breakfast?" he said.

Martha's Kitchen was about 100 yards from *The Echo*. It opened at 6:00 a.m. and was home to Oak Hills early birds. Breakfast clientele included farmhands, carpenters, clerks, teachers, and others. Today Martha's was subdued, without the banter and friendly insults usually tossed around between the morning waitress, Denise, and her regulars. Sarah sensed the mood, and left her father to his thoughts. Finally the eggs and pancakes were almost gone.

"These were good, but nobody makes pancakes like your mother," Baker said, stirring his coffee absently. "You know, anything can happen to anybody any time. That accident took about five seconds. We think we'll have time to do something we should, and then realize

it's impossible because the other person isn't there anymore. I can't help thinking about the years with your
mother and you and Georgie, Sarah. Right now I'm very
aware of what a gift they were, every minute of them.
They're treasures I'll always have."

Sarah felt then she loved her father as much as she
could ever love anybody. But the next few moments of
conversation were gone from memory when she tried to
recall them later; her mind had switched to another track.
How deep was the bond between her parents, how un-
fathomable the love! She had inherited her mother's pale
beauty and long graceful frame. She knew her father had
first loved her mother for those charms, but flowers fade
and branches bend. What remained was selflessness, understanding, courage, mirth. He had tried to love her back
the same way.

Sarah's own trophy cases in the family living room,
stuffed with medals, ribbons, and athletic icons from
school days and long for her a source of pride, glittered
less this day as the measure of a life, not much deeper
than the sprayed-on color of the figurines locked in their
airless case of glass.

"Your brother grew up in a Tigh Harbor cocoon, Sarah.
Of course lots of people did, and do. But he got out of it
fast in that torpedo boat. Every time he writes me he's
different. It's a hell of a way to have to grow up, but I'm
really proud of him, and he's serious about studying
forensics and joining the Highway Patrol when this is

over. In San Luis Obispo, of course. Amazing how Georgie's friend Janet just happens to live there! Thank God for the G.I. Bill."

Everyone else had left Martha's, and the waitress moved to empty the coffee pot into her father's cup. "No more, Denise, good lord! Might keep me awake all day." Sarah knew her father was wide-awake, and it wasn't from the coffee. She sat quietly, took in the aromas of Martha's, the formica tabletops, the brown naugahyde seats lined up like dominos along the window, then came back to the thoughtful expression on her father's face.

"It's the Ketterman girl, Sarah. I think you were fourteen, and we'd just moved to Oak Hills."

"I remember, Daddy. It was horrible."

The tragic deaths of the bus accident had called up, once again, the death of Ursula Ketterman, a brutal murder that had shaken the community to its core.

"Questions about that case have just kept coming back," Baker said. "I don't think we know the whole story. Sheriff Russell said that Kirby had messed up the footprints and tire tracks at the murder scene. That just doesn't make sense at all. Kirby's too bright to do something so stupid. Russell is Caulfield's man, of course. Bought and sold, that's no secret. And what's the connection between the girl knowing Timmy Caulfield all her life and then him dropping out of sight within a week of the murder?"

During an adolescence that seemed like forever, Sarah had been hearing of her father's conflicts with Tigh Harbor's self-proclaimed first citizen. Throughout her impressionable high school years she had been animated by it. That morning at Martha's she would discover where the animosity began, and learn a chapter of her family's story she had barely known.

Caulfield's family was old money. Baker's father was a merchant who had opened a small shop that grew before WWI to become the favorite department store of Tigh Harbor. Kenneth Caulfield was nine years older than George Baker. At age 26 Caulfield fell madly in love with a beautiful 17-year-old high school senior.

"I was also in love with that young woman, Sarah. She didn't reciprocate Caulfield's feeling for her, nor did she stay in Tigh Harbor to be with me. Instead she went away to get a college education at Berkeley. I left for college, too, to Penn State, and France during the war. When it was all over, I came home and dove into the inky pool of the newspaper business. It became a passion.

"First I got a job on *The Sentinel,* one of three papers in Tigh Harbor then: *The Sentinel,* the *Citizen-News,* and the *Patriot.* I kid you not, Sarah, sometimes I thought publishing was as bloody as war. There was lying, sabotage, spying, anything you can think of. Eventually the owner of the *Citizen-News* cut his losses by selling out to Caulfield, who promptly closed the paper down. *The Sentinel* struggled along but soon was headed for bankruptcy.

That's when I got lucky. I had been loyal to Dusty Smithson, the owner, ever since I came to his paper; now he was going to be loyal to me."

Sarah was riveted by what her father was saying; she could picture it like a movie.

"But that was only one reason for my luck. The other was that Smithson hated Caulfield like sin. Caulfield's paper had carried pictures of city street potholes he claimed were the result of shoddy construction. He didn't bother to mention that the damage was caused by broken water pipes, or by loads of bricks falling off wagons, or that a particular street was more than 35 years old. The truth was, he owned part of a company bidding for the city's street improvement contract. Dusty Smithson had originally bought *The Sentinel* as a sideline investment, a sort of hobby. But it was never his passion. His passion was roads."

"Roads?"

"Right, babe, roads and streets. Almost every street and sidewalk built in Tigh Harbor in the first two decades of the century was built by Smithson and Company. That's where Smithson and Caulfield went to war."

"That sounds like a gangster story, Daddy!"

"A junior edition. Eventually, when Smithson couldn't make a go of it with the paper, his focus turned to jabbing Caulfield. He paid off all his debts and sold me the equipment for pennies on the dollar, to deny Caulfield the satisfaction of buying out and burying another competitor. I re-launched the *Sentinel* in 1923 without skipping a single edition. We struggled at first, but we had fresh ideas and a lively editorial style, and soon we were taking bigger and bigger bites out of Caulfield's advertising revenue.

"See Dad, it's all about advertising, isn't it!"

"Well, there were personal things involved as well, and they'd also started years before. In 1919 Caulfield bought a new Pierce Arrow Raceabout. It was faster and more powerful then any machine in Keaton County. And it was the only car in town that wasn't black; it was red, with wood spoke wheels. Caulfield would drive it like he was in a race, and pedestrians, bicycles, wagons and Model-Ts just had get out of his way. It's amazing that he never killed anyone. He certainly tried, as far as I could see. It went on like that for years. Then when he got a 12-cylinder Packard in the 30s he kept doing the same thing.

"In 1938 the Police department hired this ex-Marine, Kirby, as a rookie cop. Kirby was a guy who did everything by the book and wouldn't take nonsense from anybody. He rode the department's brand new Indian motorcycle. His first week on the force he spotted Caulfield tearing down Shoreline Drive like a madman at about five in the afternoon, when lots of people were going home from work. So he went after him with his siren wailing and you could hear it all over town. Kirby finally stopped him right in front of the Court House, just as everyone was coming out.

Caulfield yelled, 'What the hell do you mean by this, young man?' and Kirby said, 'I mean by this, Sir, that you're going very much faster than is allowed here, so you're going to get a speeding citation.' Kirby didn't have any idea who Caulfield was, nor did he know that every other cop on the force had been looking the other way for years while Caulfield terrorized the town; for whatever reasons, they'd never stopped him.

"Well, Caulfield told this rookie cop off in no uncertain terms, including that he'd have his badge and do you realize who you're talking to? 'Stay right here, Mr. Caulfield,' Kirby said, and he walked across the street into the Court House, where he talked to the Chief of Police. The Chief said, 'Give him a ticket.'

"By this time a lot of folks were standing around watching, including one of your daddy's ace reporters, complete with a Speed Graphic camera, flash gun and all. Now Caulfield wasn't having any of this and roared off down the street in a rage, making people jump aside to get out of his way. Kirby came out of the Court House just in time to see the Packard disappearing around the bend. He took off after him again, siren going full blast. Next day the story and pictures were hard to miss on the *Sentinel's* front page. The war heated up from there."

"Okay, maybe not cops and robbers, but close."

"Well, we'd had another reason not to be bosom buddies, and that was probably the most important one. When that beautiful high school senior came back as a beautiful college graduate, I'd come back from that very un-beautiful war. Thank God your mother said yes to me, because that's when the best years of my life began. Caulfield had given up on Louise by then and married a socialite who had money and connections. Eventually she gave him four children. She died when he was in his forties and he married again. He was over fifty when Timothy was born."

By the time they walked out of Martha's Kitchen, Sarah knew why her father felt as he did. The disappointment of losing his paper, and the strain of starting over had all come from Caulfield's chicanery. And overlaying everything was her father's awareness that her mother had suffered from his own bitterness, however much he'd tried to mask it. He was never far from the thought that the burden of Caulfield's conniving added to all she had been forced to carry for what should have been the best years of her life. "That was harder for me than anything else," he said.

PART THREE

Back in her room since ten at the timeworn Century Hotel, Sarah was too keyed up to sleep, too distracted to lose herself in the book she'd brought along for just such moments as this. She'd called Ernie at *The Echo* and shared her excitement about finding Timothy Caulfield's grave. Her call to Martin, in hopes of reconnecting on a friendly, if not intimate basis had been unanswered. She had not expected him to be at home. The Santa Ana wind seemed to be blowing itself out. She had to shut herself down too. It was nearly midnight when she picked up the phone to call the front desk and request a wake up call. She had to let the phone ring a dozen times before the night clerk answered. Aware of a building anxiety about her morning appointment, she knew an early run would get her mind sharp and focused.

Whatever the implications of the awful scene with Martin two days ago might be, Sarah knew she was entering a different stage of her business and her life. Buying the bigger and faster press was the leap of faith she'd dreamed of and planned for ever since she'd become aware of *The Echo's* real potential; and that was thanks mostly to the support of one Mister Ernest Hemmingway. What a name! And what a talent!

Ernie seemed to be able to handle any kind of editorial

assignment, and his writing was so good she imagined he'd be getting offers from metropolitan dailies before long. But he had promised that he would see her through the expansion of *The Echo*. Hopefully Martin would get his head screwed back on and realize what a great future they could have. He was a whiz at bookkeeping and administration, and she needed that. She felt a lot less raw toward him now than she had when she'd left Oak Hills. They'd both said things that might be hard to take back, but still could be forgiven and put behind them. She put it all behind her now and went to sleep.

By 6:15 the next morning she was heading west along Santa Monica Boulevard, running easily, her pony tail triple tied with a band of white cotton yarn. She kept that pace for twenty minutes, turned around and cooled down on the return to the hotel. She trotted up three flights of stairs to her room, and refocused on the meeting coming in less than two hours. Just the thought was thrilling.

Her father had wanted this. Now she was taking the leap, and *The Echo* would be heard far and wide. She stepped into the shower, a square box with no light, but a white cloth curtain that allowed her to see the faucets. The big nozzle pointed straight down, provided little force, but nicely mimicked a waterfall. She let it run over her after she had finished washing, cooling herself down gradually until only the cold tap was on. The towels were old but clean, and she used both of them.

The offices of Frawley Cascade were a ten minute

walk from the hotel, in the first of what would apparently be a group of high rise buildings to be known as Century City. At precisely 9:58 the elevator door opened and she stepped out onto the 23rd floor. There was no corridor, only an expensive looking receptionist's desk slightly to the side, and behind it an expensive looking receptionist. Evidently the entire floor belonged to Frawley Cascade. Her appointment was with the Assistant Facilities Manager, whoever that was. She announced herself to Miss Expensive and took a seat in a designer leather chair, which was supported on a arched frame of chromed spring steel. About twenty yards in front of the elevator was the boardroom, its floor to ceiling doors open wide for maximum effect, showing off a directors' table long enough to be a bowling alley. Around the table, chairs covered in teal green were perfectly arranged.

At two minutes past nine, a Mr. Arnold Henning appeared from some inner sanctum, and introduced himself. He seemed a cold fish. Well, he was an accountant, like Martin. She followed him through a labyrinth to his office. Amazingly, it was about the size of her own, without a window. She gave quiet thanks for having escaped the corporate rock crusher. Judging from the venue provided for this great financial transaction, her purchase of the press from Frawley Cascade's Las Vegas newspaper was not causing a great ripple at the company. However, Mr. Henning did offer her coffee.

Thirty minutes later she was in the elevator, having

submitted for review the spreadsheets she'd received from Martin. She'd signed an authorization for her bank to release the company's financial information to Frawley Cascade. As the door opened at the ground level, she realized her legs were trembling, and she sat for a few minutes on a polished marble bench in the lobby.

Tomorrow she would return at midday to sign the sales contract, and not be in such a state. Frawley had the rest of the day to conduct due diligence, including getting a Dunn and Bradstreet, and the cold fish had said there should be no trouble in verifying the information before closing time. She had been talking for two months with Frawley's asset management office about this purchase, and she not only knew the price, but the inherent value of the equipment. A similar press offered for sale in Sacramento was listed for a third more than she would be paying. Thank God for the capital equipment fund her father had built. With that equity as security she would have an attractive interest rate.

She had twenty four hours to wait. From her hotel she called Ernie. He was out, interviewing the mother of a teenager killed on his motorcycle just about the hour she'd taken off from Tigh Harbor. From the typesetter who was taking calls she'd learned the accident was on the same road she'd seen from the window of the plane. The boy had owned the machine for two days, and apparently was trying to find out how fast it would go on the open road. She left a message for Ernie to call her.

Well, think of that. The first person I called was Ernie Hemmingway. Not my dearly beloved husband. Of course Martin has poured nothing but cold water over this move from the beginning. On Saturday he'd literally stuck the whole project in the deep freeze. But why on earth is he so against it? Is this such a radical move? It makes business sense, surely. Does he think we ought to be going in a different direction? Martin seems to be down on everything right now, the paper, the town, even me. So why shouldn't I call Ernie? He's supported me all along . . .

*　*　*　*

Sarah and Ernie Hemmingway first met in 1946 at a teacher's home on San Francisco Bay. In the September following her year at junior college, she'd enrolled as a sophomore at Berkeley, her mother's alma mater, declaring a major in Advertising and Public Relations. The student body startled her at first, because the men were so much older than her classmates at Tigh Harbor. Then she realized that many were veterans, their tuition paid for by the GI Bill. They were from every part of the country. On their way to the Pacific Theater during the war they had passed through California, liked it better than where they'd come from, and determined to come back if they survived. Some didn't. A lot did. They were serious in ways she hadn't experienced before. Sarah was studious but popular, helped in no small measure by her lissome figure and natural good looks. She didn't flaunt those assets and didn't need to, instead enjoyed displaying a posture of assertiveness with fellow students, and to some degree with faculty.

She thrived on competition, and ambition was her food and drink, qualities she would of course demur should someone suggest they might be her motivation. Sometimes in the early hours of the morning she would put on her warm ups and head out of her dorm at dawn, along the campus pathways, the still sleeping streets of the town, running hard, thinking hard, planning hard how to get ahead. By the Christmas holidays she had fixed her sites on the ultimate goal of owning and running an advertising agency. The objective clarified, she could now assess the relevance of all she did.

The awareness pleased her enormously; she felt it gave her a special edge. Few, if any, of her friends had settled on a career or profession, with the exception of some of the vets. She promised herself: by the time she graduated, she would complete courses in public relations, sales and marketing, psychology, and creative writing. In addition to her Spanish.

For a creative writing essay assignment about The Person Who Has Influenced You Most, Sarah wrote about her father. Four days later, Mr. McKinney read her paper to the class, to her embarrassment and secret delight.

The course was Sarah's favorite. A tight little band of aspiring writers had gravitated into the classroom of Arthur McKinney. A sometimes churlish ex-foreign correspondent, McKinney had moved to town in August,

1945, after risking his life for a number of years as a journalist on the bloody battlefields of Europe and Southeast Asia. When pressed about why he'd picked San Francisco, he would mutter that it was because he liked bridges. Those who knew him better, and there were only a few, knew that he'd opted for the beauty and tranquility of the place, as a haven where he might, just possibly, mitigate his pain. He had, indeed, received treatment, principally from Catherine Grecci, the University's assistant librarian.

The two first made eye contact on a beach one Saturday afternoon, about a month after McKinney had come to the city. He was sitting in a folding chair in the warm afternoon sunshine reading John Buchan's *Thirty Nine Steps* when an errant volleyball landed in his lap. A moment later, a slightly built girl with features that might have been Asian ran up to retrieve it.

She smiled apologetically, looked down at his book, took the missile and ran off. For the next hour he looked back and forth from the pages to the girl, with diminishing awareness of what he was reading. Eventually he folded his chair and walked along the beach past the players. When she saw him, the girl laughed, threw him the ball, and drew him into the game.

She warmed him like sunshine. He asked her to join him for coffee after the game. Catherine, whose mother was Thai, was smart and intuitive. Somehow she divined that gold was buried beneath McKinney's crusty exterior.

During the months that followed, their relationship passed through attraction, shared interests and experiences, to love and shared living quarters. They rented the top floor of the home of an orchid grower. It was in a little world of its own, on a bluff above a beach that was not private, but so remote as to be frequented only by the residents of the four houses nearby.

To reach the house from the town required passing through a gate and taking a gravel road past several large greenhouses. A stand of enormous eucalyptus rose along the north side of the road, and Monarch butterflies by the thousands would land in them during migrations. Orchids in endless variety grew around the house and pool. A zigzag path led down to the beach, framed from the windows by a dozen towering palms. Catherine called it Little Hawaii. McKinney called it Shangri-La.

Early in their relationship she had suggested McKinney query the university's communications department about teaching a course in writing. The university lost no time in piggybacking it's curriculum onto McKinney's fame as a correspondent, and his class was an instant success, both for the talent it discovered and its emotional benefit for the instructor.

Some Fridays, on the spur of the moment, McKinney would invite his students to drop by for a beer. Pizza would be ordered from Giovanni's, and every student who didn't have some life or death reason not to would be sure to turn up. Friday with McKinney was *the* time of the week, and usually lasted well into Saturday. The orchid grower and his wife liked the events and sometimes joined in. There, Catherine was not the demure librarian who showed up at the university on Mondays.

At the McKinneys one friday in mid December, Ernie Hemmingway, a fellow student, told Sarah that he had been impressed by her paper that was read to the class, and asked her to tell him about her father. Hemmingway was gifted and competent, and Sarah was only too glad to sing her father's praises to him. An animated discussion about reporters and correspondents had developed in the class that evening. Several of the students believed they would write the Great American Novel. Only a few were headed for journalism, let alone advertising or public relations. After a spirited hour, McKinney told them he had something personal to say. They were instantly quiet. McKinney never said anything personal.

"It's about the Fourth of July," McKinney said, and a few chuckled. For a minute, maybe more, the only sound was from waves on the sands below. McKinney sat looking at his hands. He told them then about the longest night of his life. It was 1944, only two years earlier. Between sundown of July 3rd and sunrise of July 4th, McKinney lay in a shallow depression in the blood red soil of Saipan in the Marianas Islands. He shared the spot with three 19-year-old Marines of the 4th division who had paid their last full measure of devotion. Rain was falling in torrents. Only because he was able to cover himself with their still warm bodies, did he avoid detection by the Japanese patrol that had ambushed them. After the soldiers moved on, he extracted himself, shaking, and made his way by first light, then by the fiery red dawn of the Fourth of July, to safety.

"Whether you're a dead correspondent or a live novelist doesn't matter for shit, people, unless you're living or dying for something you believe in. What you believe in and do with it is what everything is all about. We're different, all of us, different as different can be. You'll never hear my drummer and I'll never hear yours. But so what? If one drummer bangs so much better than all the other drummers in the world, why isn't everybody in lockstep right behind him? The point is, you gotta do something with your life."

They sat for several minutes then, no one speaking, staring at a log in the fireplace until it crumbled, sending sparks up the chimney. Catherine came across the room to McKinney, put her arms around him, and there were tears in her eyes. After a few minutes, several people got up to use the bathroom. Some went out to the patio to smoke or look at the bay in spite of the chill. Only Sarah and Hemmingway remained, leaning against the sofa, their legs stretched out toward the fire.

"Your father would have agreed with that," Ernie said eventually. "He would have understood McKinney, too."

"You think so?"

"I do. You said his credo was Real People, Real Lives, Real News."

"My God, you remember that?"

"Of course. You wrote a great essay. It introduced a person you'd want to meet, and if you were going to be a journalist, whom you'd want to learn from."

"Well, if I'd really written how I feel, you'd accuse me of having an Electra complex. When my mother died, my father was everything. And then I found I loved what he did as well. I wonder if I'd be in med school if he'd been a doctor."

They sat silent for a time. "The next chapter will be the most interesting," Ernie said.

"What's that?"

"That's when you tell about yourself."

Sarah looked over at him, actually seeing him now. "I've never been good at that."

Hemmingway was four years older than Sarah. He had yellow-brown hair, was tall, quite lean, self effacing, and usually kept himself in the background. At off-campus discussions over beer or coffee Ernie said little. Sarah voiced opinions. As a result, male students could easily engage her in conversation, and not infrequently connect. As long as she felt she was carrying the ball, she enjoyed the game. Ernie quietly suffered when he saw her leave with someone she just met. But he made no advances.

Now Sarah was aware that her face was flushed, and she wondered for an instant whether it was the admission she's just made or something else. "Tell me, Mr. Jamaica, now that we've been in the same class for two years, how'd you get the impossible name, Ernest Hemming-way? And don't say your daddy wrote *For Whom the Bell Tolls*."

"No, my father wasn't a writer, but he read everything and couldn't resist calling me Ernest. There's no connection to the author apart from father's literary aspirations for me. The name isn't even spelled the same. Hard to live it down, though."

"Then don't." Sarah countered. "Live it up. You're the best writer in this class. You could produce anything."

Ernie chuckled. "You have an upbeat approach to everything, Sarah. That must have come from your father." Others returned to the fireside then. A week later Sarah went home for Christmas vacation. She told her father about the progress of her classes, and that a student named, would you believe, Ernie Hemmingway, had asked about him. "He's the best writer in the class," she said. "A nice guy, too."

One night near the end of their senior year Ernie walked Sarah home the long way from McKinney's. They had hitched rides to the house with others, but it was a beautiful night, and they both enjoyed the outdoors. She pressed him to tell her about his growing up.

He was born in Jamaica, where his father had been the senior accountant on a large plantation that exported tropical fruits to Europe. During World War II all the production had been commandeered by the British Navy for His Majesty's warships. Ernie's education was British, in a small school existing exclusively for the children of the plantation owners, staff and laborers. Three fourths of the students were Jamaicans of Negro descent, and black and white equally considered themselves Jamaican. The plantation owners were third generation. After Ernie had "matriculated" he worked four years on the plantation, living at home, saving his money. He drove a 1935 English-built Ford Ferguson diesel tractor, cleared weeds and hauled boxes of fruit to the warehouses.

When he wasn't on the tractor Ernie was reading. He shamelessly boasted to Sarah that he devoured every book on the plantation, and to his parents everlasting delight, told them he'd like to write stories himself one day. He told Sarah that one night, after hours on the tractor, when his mind had soared a good part of the day into the blue skies of finding a perfect love, he'd written down a story that he'd never read to anybody. It was all about stars, and how on the night you find true love there'd be a million of them up there above you and you'd be able to count them. No, Sarah, you can't see it. Nobody's ever seen it. Ernie's uncle, his mother's brother, who owned a modestly successful men's clothing store in Palo alto, had sponsored his emigration to California.

The walk home took nearly three hours, but time passed quickly. By the direct path the distance was just a couple of miles. They talked, laughed, teased and barely touched. Sarah went to bed at about 3:00 a.m. and her thoughts were a mixture.

Well that was different. We were in some really out-of-the-way places, and he did nothing more than take my arm to help me step over a stick or something. Is he honestly that shy? Or maybe he isn't shy at all. I was ready for him not to be tonight. I think I told him more about myself than I've ever told anyone. Maybe it's the accent. Those old-world manners are beautiful. But I wanted him to touch me tonight. I really did. I know he's interested. He's interested, and I'm interested. One thing I know for sure; he's someone I can trust.

By the end of the senior year, Ernie had a scholarship awaiting him in the Master's program at Northwestern, and Sarah had signed up to work for two years in Europe with the Marshall Plan. At the close of the graduation ceremony, everyone was laughing, crying, hugging and saying good-bye. Sarah gave Ernie a long hug and then, after he looked into her eyes for a moment, he kissed her, which sent a jolt of electricity all through her. Wow, Ernie – she began to smile, so did he, then other grads came up to say their good-byes.

PART FOUR

Sarah's Century Hotel room phone rang just after noon, and it was Ernie returning her call. "How'd it go?" he asked.

"Well, we've mortgaged the farm. I never imagined I could be that nervous. The guy at Frawley is just a bean counter, but he somehow made me feel I was claiming more beans than I own. Guess I'm just not used to paying a fortune for a toy. I go back there in the morning to sign the papers."

"Yes, this is certainly an enormous step Sarah. You're moving into a bigger league now, but with this equipment you'll be able to handle contract printing from anyone. That press should be kept humming night and day, and when it's paid for, those jobs will only cost you paper, ink and labor. It's a sound investment."

"Thanks for that. Wish I had half as much support from Martin." She told Ernie she'd call him again after the signing, before she left for Las Vegas to finalize details and make shipping arrangements for the press.

"This afternoon I'm taking a cab to Santa Monica to run on the beach." Ernie, she knew, would produce two columns, check the progress of reporter assignments, and review the advertising hold for Friday's edition before he left the office for the night. He'd also be writing a story about the boy who'd been killed on the motorcycle. In the midst of all his responsibilities, he'd do it sensitively, she knew.

"Hey, guy," she said, with only a slight feeling of guilt, "If there are galley slaves, there's gotta be a slavemaster somewhere." Ernie laughed. Yes, obviously, he was her partner.

And there it is again. Why is Ernie your partner and Martin not? Dammit Martin, what's happened to you? Dad desperately wanted to do what we're doing now. He wrote about it a dozen times in letters to me in Paris...

* * * *

During her stint with the Marshall Plan in Europe, Sarah received a letter from her father nearly ever week. They were never tomes, but brief and chatty, and she relished the images they gave her, not only of him but of the innocence of small town America. Innocence until the murder of Ursula Ketterman. She'd read her roommates a few of the letters with her father's concerns about how the murder case was being handled, and read them also to Armand LeSavoie, an aristocratic-looking Geneva-born translator who was fluent in six languages and had studied international law at Zurich University.

"C'est la vie," Armand had opined, little intrigued by the application of the American justice system in a small California town. Near the end of her second year in Paris, Sarah and Armand–by then she'd dubbed him *Monsieur Le Conte*–had became more than friends. He suggested they move in together for her final eight weeks; why not split a rent? How very continental, she'd answered with a smile. "Armand, I'm going home in November."

* * * *

Sarah's first job after returning from Europe was with Northwest Allied, the Oregon-based hardware chain. She'd responded to an ad in *Public Relations* for an energetic take-charge person to help redefine the company's corporate image. There had been a lot of competition for the job, and she'd won it, despite having little business experience, and because of no end of self confidence. Her success at Allied by the end of her first year had brought her to the notice of Huntington Forest Products, Allied's largest client, and Huntington had hired her away and nearly doubled her salary. It had been heady stuff, and the thought of it still was, even now.

She had traveled a lot, mostly west of the Mississippi, and at the beginning, that was one of the most attractive parts of her job. She'd had the title of product specialist for nineteen months, and was satisfied she'd given Huntington its money's worth, putting "sizzle in the story." Not that she'd earned a fortune, even if it was twice what she'd made in Oregon. And that's what had rankled her.

Sarah knew by the volume of business she brought in that she'd produced for the company, but in spite of her title, her name on the door and her reserved parking space, she was still just a cog on the corporate wheel.

J. Walter Thompson has enjoyed a lucrative advertising contract with Huntington for twenty years. Partly from curiosity, Sarah had looked at where JWT placed ads and publicity material and found overlaps. The savings to Huntington from this discovery had earned her a fat bonus, which she was very pleased with until she calculated the bottom line benefit of her work for the company–nearly half a million. All of which came from capturing just an extra half point of Weyerhaeuser's marketplace hegemony. There was so much money in business! But she didn't own the agency, and if she didn't own her own business, she didn't own her life.

Sarah had been on the road to entrepreneurship since she could remember. Wasn't that a principle she'd learned from her father? All her life he'd never worked for anyone else. It wasn't his nature and it wasn't hers. She didn't just like to be in charge. She had to be. And then, suddenly, she was.

* * * *

She remembered that morning two years ago. The rain still hadn't stopped when she'd opened her eyes. Was it really morning? Who could tell? Anyway, it was Saturday, and she didn't have to be anywhere. This was a day to play catch up in her apartment. You don't need sunshine for that. Tacoma is beautiful to visit in the summer, which was on a Wednesday last year. No, that's not fair. The Northwest is a great big garden, and gardens need water. That's why we've got all these wonderful trees, and why Huntington Forest Products is so rich. There were gorgeous moments this winter, too; she may have been out of town those days. When she was in Tacoma she ran less than she used to, because she didn't like drizzle and rainy streets.

* * * *

But Dad's paper was doing well. Sarah was delighted that he was so thrilled about going countywide. It will be such a joy for him; he's always worked hard. And now, incredibly, Ernie Hemmingway is there. What a support that must be! Ernie is the greatest writer. But how on earth did he end up in Oak Hills? I guess it was through some professor. I thought Ernie would be with a big city paper by this time. Well, Dad will have a big city story now diving back into the Ketterman murder. Don't know how many times he's written, and talked about it on the phone. He got pretty ticked off when Georgie refused even to discuss it. Not like Georgie at all. But Dad had always thought the case was bogus; too many coincidences, too many loose ends. Where did Timothy Caulfield go? Were the sheriff and the judge bought and paid for? "I've made a big decision, Sarah," he'd said. "I'm going to investigate the case."

Sarah had been hearing about the Ketterman murder

for nearly half her lifetime. Now it was clear the killer was still on the loose, and that was a scary thought. She should schedule a visit to Oak Hills. It had been six months since she'd been able to give her father a hug. She'd finally roused herself, splashed water on her face and plugged in her coffee maker when the phone rang.

Oh heck. This is Saturday. She let it ring and went into the bathroom. After eight rings the caller hung up, then rang again. Reluctantly, Sarah answered with "Hello?' then heard the urgent voice of her brother, now with the California Highway Patrol in San Luis Obispo, whom she hadn't seen for a year. At his first words, she froze.

"Sarah, Dad's had a heart attack–"

"What? Georgie! How is he? Is he okay?"

"He's in the hospital, Sis. I don't really know yet. I got a radio call about two hours ago when I was still out on patrol. I talked to Ernie and learned Dad had been in his room at the paper. He got downstairs to call for help. Don't know the details. The hospital wouldn't tell me much. I'm leaving now, and should be there by noon."

"I'll get a plane as soon as I can. Oh dear God, Daddy, don't go, don't go."

"He's at Mercy, Sarah, I'll see you there."

"Give him all my love, Georgie, and hug him, hug him, hug him." There was a plane leaving in 90 minutes, and Sarah raced to catch it. No traffic tickets, but no extra clothes or makeup either, not even a toothbrush. Her flight connected at San Jose to a commuter that would land in Tigh Harbor at 12:30. She couldn't eat the cold sandwich offered on the first leg of the flight, but the coffee was life-giving. She looked out the window the whole way. It was eerie in the extreme to be landing in the town she had lived in during her childhood, knowing that she was coming to see the person she loved most in all the world, and he was struggling for his life. She tried not to think about it, preferring numbness to mask the fear. What would life be without her father? She'd never asked that before, never wanted to even consider the possibility.

* * * *

The plane landed and she walked down the steps and crossed the tarmac toward the terminal. The bougainvillea-covered arches were where they were supposed to be, but the color seemed to have drained from the blossoms.

"Sarah."

She turned and Ernie was standing there in a blue shirt. For a split second she was back at graduation in Berkeley. She threw her arms around him and cried.

Ernie said little during the drive up the Ridge Road except that her father appeared to be stabilizing, and was getting the best care possible. When the attack had come, he had managed to get to the top of the stairway and literally slid down.

At the hospital her father was awake and responding to

treatment. He talked for a minute or two with Sarah and Georgie. Then the nurse said that was enough, and the two drove to the house, to get some food and talk about what to do next. Ernie went to the paper.

Brother and sister returned to their father's bedside that afternoon, evening and the following morning. He seemed better each time. After lunch Georgie drove back to San Luis Obispo. Sarah spent much of the next three days with her father at Mercy, then brought him home. She cooked dinner for him, set him up by the fireplace in his recliner with a throw over his feet, and generally fussed about him.

"Pretty nice," said the patient, grinning wryly. "Your mother cooked great meals too, but then she kicked me out the door to bring home some more bread and butter. Thanks for being here, Sarah."

"I'll always be here when you need me, Daddy."

"Well then listen to me now, Sarah. I've got something important to talk about with you. And it's not just the result of a heart attack, although that makes it pretty immediate. I want you to take over the paper."

Sarah gasped. "Are you serious?"

"No, back that up. I'm *asking* you if you'd like to take over the paper, be willing to take it over, dare to take it over, however you want to put it. I'd thought I'd be talking with you about this after we'd expanded, because I think you'd have considered that a worthier offer. But this seems the best time, considering everything. I know the plan to go countywide will work. Georgie thinks so, too, even if *The Echo* isn't on his radar. You've got the talent and the pizzazz to pull it off, and you'd have the satisfaction of doing something bigger than your old man ever did."

"Oh Daddy, you can do anything. I know you can. You're equipped better than I'll ever be. Besides, you've got years and years ahead of you."

"Well, maybe so. But if you're going to have a changing of the guard, it's a good idea to do it while the King is still in the palace." He laughed and smiled a little smile. "Think about it, Sarah. Think about it."

By the time she was ready to fly back to Tacoma, Sarah had thought about it, discussed it, researched it, even prayed about it. Her father had been making great strides in his recovery, and they'd talked at length every day. She had promised him an answer before she left. She made her decision before breakfast on her last morning.

She had been wakened by the sunrise on her face, found her track suit from college, which she was pleased to discover still fit, and headed out of town. Running, as always, seemed to clear her mind and give her focus. Four miles past the bottling plant after the houses thinned, the old Scotch church rose up in the distance, just as she remembered it.

If she were to take on *The Echo*, however, nothing

would be as she remembered it. She'd no longer be the free young thing, cavorting over the countryside with Elena, stopping to look at a beetle walking on its nose, laughing at the comedy of a line of quail running for cover, skinny dipping in the lake by Papa Beto's field. She'd have the responsibilities of building a business that was her own. Just the thought generated fear, but more than that, a thrill. The editorial side of the paper seemed to be in good hands with Ernie on board, at least for the foreseeable future. Her father had brought in a new business manager. She'd looked at all the pitfall possibilities she could think of, and couldn't find any problem that was greater than the potential gain of taking the risk. And she could create an advertising agency, independent from the paper, that would service the needs not only of the paper's clients, but the whole region. It would be her own business.

Her father had told her he thought Ernie was exceptional, and she had been quick to agree. On the first day he'd been allowed by the doctor, Hemmingway had visited the hospital and volunteered to stay on through the expansion project.

"You can't imagine the security that is to me," her father had said. "He'd only come on board for a year. Now he'll have a lot more to do. He ought to have the use of the apartment. I won't need it anymore, won't be keeping those hours."

The financial side of the paper was being handled by

Martin Daniels, *The Echo's* business manager. Baker had found him through an ad in *Editor and Publisher.* Daniels was a CPA and had owned a business in Kansas City. Apparently he'd had enough of self-employment in the midwest and wanted to move to California. Baker had checked his references and taken him on. For several months Daniels had been paying receivables and handling *The Echo's* accounting, tasks her father had never enjoyed.

Sarah didn't enjoy those tasks either, in spite of the fact that owning a business was her dream. She was a bottom line person, with little patience for details, and no patience at all for minutiae. If Martin was the man her father had picked to handle the finances, that was good enough for her. More than good enough, in fact; the guy was good looking. He reminded her of Tyrone Power, her mother's favorite movie star. Hollywood was all about fantasy, of course, but if you're going to work with somebody, it wouldn't do any harm if he's okay to look at.

"So the paper's really solid financially?" she'd asked Martin.

"Very. Your father's a savvy man about business, even if he doesn't want to handle its details. He's built up a capital improvement fund of nearly $150 thousand, and an operating fund that he's been adding to for years. The company is healthy, and it's all due to George's business smarts. He used an accounting firm in Tigh Harbor before he brought me in. He's been acting as editor, publisher and general manager all at the same time, and it was too much. He knew he'd need business management help for the expansion."

"Well, if I come aboard I certainly will, Martin. I'm a lot like my father, pretty bottom line."

"A lot prettier bottom line, if I may say so."

"Hey, you, you're supposed to stick to figures."

"I am."

They both laughed. She knew she liked the flirting.

Baker beamed with delight when Sarah told him at breakfast of her decision to take on the paper. Her big brother had opted for a different kind of career, and had no interest in publications. But Sarah was a chip off her daddy's block, and in addition to her talents, she had the drive that he regarded as a quality beyond price. At breakfast she told him she would need eight weeks to make the move from Washington, to train her replacement and keep doing her job.

"Sarah, you've really put some salt in my oats," Baker exclaimed. "There'll be great days ahead."

She told Ernie her decision as he drove her to the airport. "Betcha never thought anything like this would happen, did you, Ernie?"

His look was enigmatic. "Not this soon, anyway," he answered. "But your father and I have talked over a lot of things these past months, and this was one of his dreams.

He wants the best for you, Sarah. He knew you'd be a success in whatever you did, but hoped above everything else that you could be with him in the business. You must have made him very happy."

"I hope it's a happy thought for you, Ernie. I know you weren't planning to stay here for eternity, but I'm going to be leaning on your everlasting arms a lot now." Watching the familiar countryside pass by her window, she failed to notice the look on Ernie's face.

In Tacoma five days later she had a lengthy afternoon meeting with Huntington's Sales Director and Ethan Williams, the company's Executive Vice President, who tried multliple incentives to convince her to stay, including a major salary increase and stock options. Thank you, but no thanks, she said. She'd been honored to work with Huntington, yet she was decided. She would leave in sixty days, but would first properly train her replacement.

She had dinner that evening with her best friend in the company. Marilyn Collins had two sons in their late twenties and was technically the office receptionist, although Sarah had become aware in her first week at Huntington that it was she who made the office work. The engineers, marketers and product managers had the titles, but Marilyn set the tone for the place. "If you were ever working for me, young lady," Sarah said over a dinner of wild Coho salmon, "I'd call you the Company Liaison Officer and give you stock." Marilyn's husband worked for a fastener company that made fittings for

Boeing. "When you and Fred get some time off, come see me. You guys will love my dad. We've got plenty of room, and you hardly ever hear an airplane."

As she unlocked her apartment door just before 8 o'-clock she heard her telephone. It was Ernie. He gave her the sorrowful news that less than an hour earlier her father had died of a stroke at home. She stayed on the line with Ernie until after nine, parts of the hour just being quiet.

Tightly holding her emotions in check, Sarah flew back once again to Oak Hills, where with her brother she arranged for the funeral. The most beautiful flowers in the packed old Scotch church were from Elena and her parents. Eighteen of the Cardenas family attended the service. Elena flew home from Chicago, where she was interning as a heart surgeon at Lakeshore Memorial, a hospital dating back to the Civil War. She sat next to Sarah during the service.

That evening, in the now hollowed Baker home on the edge of town, Sarah wept with her brother and Janet, his wife, and did her best to console her father's three grand-children. Next morning she talked briefly with Martin and Ernie about *The Echo's* affairs, then flew back to Tacoma to wrap up her job and move to Oak Hills.

* * * *

The first hundred days at *The Echo* were frantic, a goulash of emotions, work, uncertainties, learning, revi-

sions, and not a whole lot of fun. Only her pride kept
Sarah from admitting how badly she needed to unwind.
She'd been doing her best to dig into the business, with
Martin about accounting, with Ernie about the editorial
side of the paper. She knew of no precedent for what she
was experiencing; a woman not as a society reporter but
in management? A woman owner of a newspaper? One
Thursday evening after the deadlines she sat with Ernie
in the quiet office and talked for hours, exploring implications of the expansion that she had until now considered only superficially. Ernie had a feel for what her
father had hoped to achieve. One of his comments surprised her.

"He was rethinking his perspective on Kenneth
Caulfield, I believe," Ernie said. "After his heart attack
he spent less time at the office of course, but he came in
most days. I'd drop by the house to see him in the
evenings. He wanted to know how everything was going.
I really thought he was getting stronger.

"A few days before he died he told me a lot about your
mother, and how thrilled he'd been when she'd said yes
to him 'way back when.' I guess Caulfield had courted
her once. Then he talked about Caulfield's family, his
first wife who died, his children, their children. He
showed me Caulfield's book with a big photo of the family in it. I got the sense he was reaching for something–
some place–in his mind, I couldn't say what."

"Maybe it was Heaven, Ernie. Mother always went to

church, and most of the time she took us with her. When she was gone, Daddy and I just spent our Sundays together. It was a kind of church, I guess."

"If it really was Heaven he was looking for, I think he found it, Sarah. That last evening when I came over he was sitting in front of the fire, and I don't think I'd ever seen him look so contented. Wherever he was, he was in a wonderful place. He'd been with the Cardenas's for dinner and they'd laughed all through the meal about how unfair it was that you couldn't choose your neighbors if they'd got there first. They'd brought him home just 30 minutes before I found him."

Yes, Sarah thought, he's in a wonderful place, but that doesn't mean I miss him any less. "I'm so glad it was you, Ernie. I would hate it if someone who didn't mean anything to him had found him. You were just destined to be with my father, I guess. I still don't understand how some professor put you two together. Tell me."

One of the classmates of Sarah's father at Columbia had been Arnold Jewison. After graduation Baker and Jewison had gone to work for different papers. Twenty years later, when Jewison was at the Atlanta Constitution, he decided he wanted to train journalists. He would become a teacher. At Northwestern he taught media ethics and media and the law.

"He was my mentor, Sarah. I probably learned more from Professor Jewison than from anyone else. He said I could certainly find a job with a major paper, but there would be a risk for me in that."

"Ha, you don't think coming here was a risk?"

"Ask me in my next life, Sarah. No, Jewison was different. He'd look at a student in a number of ways; first as an individual, then as a type of individual, and only then as a journalist. He told me I risked not understanding where people were living."

"C'mon, Ernie, you're probably the most understanding person I know."

"Well, frankly, I wasn't too pleased by his remark. I asked him what he meant, and he said that a phlegmatic sort of person tends to take things as they come. Some people make it happen, I tend to let it happen."

"Yes, I can remember at least one instance of that."

"But that's not bad," Ernie continued, either missing or ignoring the innuendo, "if you're aware of its positives and negatives. He just wanted to be sure I wouldn't automatically accept the culture of a big city paper. He said that when journalists focus on exceptional events or victims, as we do for hard news, we're focusing on what is not happening to most people. Of course, people want to read about exceptional things, he was very aware of that. But he made us think.

"He said if I'd be willing to spend a year in the grass roots, 'boonies' is what he called them, it would stand me in good stead when I become the most famous journalist in the world. He put me in touch with your father."

"But how did he know about *The Echo*?"

"Those two had been writing letters back and forth ever since Columbia. Professor Jewison knew that when your father took the paper countywide he'd need help."

Ernie had certainly provided the help George Baker needed. After her father died, Ernie had taken over editorial direction along with his managing editor functions and the paper hadn't skipped a beat. *The Echo* was going ahead in fine style. Everything important in town and in most of the county was being covered by two cub reporters fresh out of journalism school. Yet Sarah still felt driven to prove herself.

* * * *

On Friday evening a week later, Sarah's desk was covered with accounting sheets. Every column she looked at seemed to increase her strain. The week's edition had been delivered that afternoon, a few calls had come in to her desk, especially about the editorial on the need for a better working relationship between the council and City Manager John Shaw, and the callers had promised to write letters to the editor. Ernie had left at noon on a three day sail to the Channel Islands with Will Carlisle, his tennis buddy and a partner in the law firm that had represented *The Echo* since her father moved to Oak Hills. The papers on her desk were P&Ls, accounting details, and estimates for the balance of 1954.

"Martin, do accountants really understand the stuff they throw at regular people?"

"Believe it or not, they do, Sarah. And believe it or not, CPAs are regular people too; they just speak a different language."

Martin had brought her spreadsheets she'd requested because she wanted to take them home for the weekend. He had volunteered to stay late to explain them to her shortly after he'd learned that Ernie would be away at the Islands. *Yes, our pretty little publisher has kept her nose to the grindstone most weekends since she flew in here, and while it hasn't made her any less cute, I'm not being paid to work seven days a week. Who knows? She certainly doesn't like handling accounts.*

"With a little practice the language gets understandable, Sarah. Doesn't even need translation. It's just that it's numbers instead of letters. But of course that's what accountants and business managers go to college to learn. Your father hired me to do all that kind of stuff for him."

"Thank God for that, Martin. He obviously had confidence in you." Sarah rocked back in her father's old desk chair and stretched, flexing her shoulders to relieve the stiffness. She seemed unaware that the motion pulled her blouse against her chest. Martin was not unaware.

"You're tense, Sarah. You need to loosen up." He stood and moved behind her, then very lightly pushed on the muscles above her shoulders.

"Oh, that's good. Funny, I was just thinking the same thing. To be honest, I've not really been following these spreadsheets very well. I never like to admit things, but I guess I'm just kinda tired." She closed her eyes.

"Sure you are. So relax a bit. I'm pretty good at this." He was, indeed. Expert, in fact. He kneaded the tensed up muscles across her shoulders. Talking quietly about work and weather and nothing in general, Martin gradually moved down the muscles in her back. She didn't object. He massaged her head, moving slowly from her neck to her forehead. He eased her head against his body, gently held her there with his left hand beneath her chin. With his right he worked the muscles of her upper arm, then all of her arm to the tip of each finger. He switched hands and did the same on the other side.

"Oh, that feels good."

"It's supposed to."

He took her arm again, this time holding it to her side, so that his hand and fingers grazed her body as he went lower. When he was at her fingertips, and her hand was in her lap, he made it linger there, pressing ever so lightly against the Y at the top of her legs.

Sarah knew full well what was happening. From the first touch. And it took her only a moment to realize she welcomed it. After her dalliances at Berkeley and the foreign affair in Paris, she had kept her sex life under control. She was desirable, she knew; men always made it obvious. But she'd determined to avoid any serious relationship. *A cast iron lid on everything, Sarah.*

She lifted her hand from her lap and reached back to grasp Martin's leg. Then did the same with her other hand. She pulled him toward her and laid her cheek against his chest. His hands slid down her body to her breasts. She looked up and invited his kiss.

She led him to her father's tiny room upstairs. It had no personality. no pictures, no flowers, just a narrow bed. They made love in the glow from the light that spilled up the stairs. Neither tore the clothes off the other. Afterward, Sarah felt tears in her eyes, from passion, certainly, but even more from simply feeling alive.

They lay there until Martin turned and said, "Do you know that I've loved you from the moment your father told me about you?"

"What?"

"It's true, Sarah. We were closing the books on the first month I was here. George seemed so happy to have my help. 'Someday maybe you'll be doing this for Sarah,' he said to me. That was the first time he'd mentioned you. I still remember the tone in his voice. Having you here was his dream. Don't ask me how it happened, Sarah, but from everything he told me about you, you became my dream too. When I saw you months later, I realized why."

Stunned, Sarah turned her head to the man beside her.

81

His features were rimmed by the light from the stairway, a handsome profile. He looked relaxed, sure of himself, qualities she admired. *Sarah, imagine! I'm lying in Daddy's bed and just been with Daddy's man and I feel wonderful.*

"I never knew, Martin. And I'm touched. But right now I guess I'm coming out of a tunnel. I don't know what to say."

"No need to say anything, Sarah." He reached across her waist to her side. Soon she turned to him.

When Martin got to his apartment that night at 2:15 a.m., he slipped into bed beside a long sleek body. The girl murmured, turned toward him and stretched her arm across his chest.

"Hi, baby," she said.

"Hi doll, it's late."

"Sure it is baby, and you're all pooped out. Here, let me take care of everything."

* * * *

Events that impacted the life of Ernest Hemmingway, be they distressing, disgusting or delightful, were usually homogenized in the sizable lake of his obliging personal-

82

ity. On the Monday morning after his Channel Islands getaway, Ernie came into the office with a Cheshire grin, a reddish weekend tan and an embellished story of sailing three hours on a broad reach in a 20 knot wind.

"Sorry, landlubbers, but we had all the ballast we needed." He laughed and Sarah and Martin laughed too, but with restraint.

"Well, some can tell 'em and some can't," Ernie said. "Let's look at the week."

Staff meetings took place on Monday morning, to crank up from the weekend. Everyone knew the working schedule of a weekly was a luxury compared with the relentless intensity of a big city daily, and they treated the pace as a perk. Features for the coming issue had been assigned days earlier, and Monday was principally the time to review current news and try to divine what might break before this week's deadline. Conversation was usually interspersed with banter and off-the-subject comments. This morning it was subdued, Ernie noted. Well, not everybody had a sailing weekend.

In the afternoon he had another meeting with Sarah about the expansion. To start with, they would increase editorial coverage in the three smaller towns up on the mesa, focusing initially on the quality of the education available for elementary school children. Each town had its own grade school. Junior high and high school students were bussed to Oak Hills.

"You grew up here, Sarah," Ernie said after the meeting to his publisher, whom he thought seemed preoccupied today. "How old were you when you came?"

"I was 13. My grade school days were all in Tigh Harbor. When you're just barely a teenager you can't imagine ever leaving where you live. But we were moving house, not just getting bussed to school. It'll be different for all these kids. I was losing my friends. They'll have all their friends coming with them."

"Must have been a big upheaval for you. Your mother was already ill then, wasn't she?"

"Yes, but I didn't realize how seriously sick she was. I knew she'd fallen a few times, and had lost some sensation in her fingers. But I was more concerned about leaving my friends. It tears me up when I think about that now. I wasn't even aware that when she hugged me her fingers couldn't feel me. Daddy was a saint. They kept things as normal as they could be for the longest time. When I began to understand how sick she was I started doing a lot more to help. These things only get to you later, when you see what your parents have done for you, the sacrifices they made. And they loved making them, that's what's amazing, Ernie. So they weren't really sacrifices at all. More like love offerings." She was quiet then, her eyes lowered, and said, "I want that family."

Before Ernie could respond the phone rang. The following days unrolled as usual. On Friday, Sarah told Martin that she was tired and would get an early night.

"Call me at the office on Saturday," he said. "I'll be here by midday."

Martin was alone when the phone rang. Ernie had gone for a round of golf.

"Hi," Sarah said. "How ya doin'?

"I'll be doing better when I can see you. I've missed you this week."

"Missed me? C'mon, we've been in the same office all day every day."

"Yes, and I'm the poor kid who works in the candy store and can't have any."

"Rascal. It would rot your teeth. How about supper? I make a mean lasagna."

"That would be nice. Maybe we could even have dessert."

She had the table set by the west window, with candles. They flirted with each other, and Martin teased her until she blushed. They left everything on the table when she took his hand and led him to the bedroom. When she came back two hours later to make coffee, the candles had burned down to the holders, spilling melted wax onto the mats beneath. In the future she must remember to put something under them.

By the next week, Ernie realized that between Martin and Sarah there was more than a business connection. He could do nothing but watch it grow stronger until, four weeks later, Sarah announced to *The Echo* staff that she and Martin were engaged to be married.

The news virtually bent Ernie in two, like a hammer badly wielded bends a nail. He had been saddened by the relationship he had seen developing, but the engagement took him completely off guard. He had not honestly confronted the fact that he was in love with this bright, ambitious girl he knew in college, had laughed with, shared aspirations with, been immensely attracted to but had only kissed good-bye on graduation day.

Hemmingway saw this as one more evidence that life just happens. It always had. He wasn't being fatalistic, he rationalized; it was just the way life was. Growing up in Jamaica, there were things to do and you did them. It had not occurred to him to try to change his circumstances or look for options. He had a big wide world in his mind, and every book he had read after his day on the tractor had taken him into that world. He'd dreamed that one day he might write about it, those people, those places, those experiences, but he didn't expect he would ever touch them, feel them, experience them himself. Dream life was vicarious. You took events around you as they came.

The plantation school in Jamaica had 52 students. Thirteen were light skinned, four of those were girls, and only two were anywhere near his age. One of the girls was attractive, the other plain. The plain girl's desk was directly behind him. When he was just sixteen and she eighteen, she began leaning forward to whisper teases in his ear, images of secret pleasures that aroused him almost uncontrollably right there underneath the algebra book on his lap.

As usual in Jamaica, the weather was warm and humid. At the end of the week they went after school to the plantation supply building, where no one would be at that hour, and where the jute sacking material used for shipping coconuts and vegetables was stored. Ernie had slipped in there once before, after working 18 hours hauling produce, and gone to sleep. A workman had wakened him ten hours later, and when he announced himself at home, his family had laughed. The sacking formed a rough mattress, and there, with the girl, Ernie came of age. He had been thrilled by it, of course, but typically had not initiated any more encounters. The girl took care of that. She went away to college the next year and never came back.

Obviously there was no future for him now with Sarah. Had she been the real reason he came to work for *The Echo*? Of course she was. If so, there was no rationale now to stay. In any case, staying would bring nothing but torment. He had come for a year, and then he'd told Baker he'd stay to prepare for the expansion. But everything was different now. Sarah would have to understand his need to move on. It was time to update his resume.

* * * *

Ernie wasn't the only one upset by Sarah's liaison with her business manager. Soon after Martin had come to work for the paper, Linda Demeter, his glamorous girl-friend from Kansas City, moved into his Oak Hills apart-ment. No stranger to California, she had spent her late teens with her aunt in Culver City, after her mother's boyfriend back in Kansas had started turning mother and daughter into a package deal. In Oak Hills she quickly got a job as a leggy cocktail waitress at the Sundowner, the town's one lounge with table service, and its only recognition that the town might have a night life. Their relationship was quickly cracked, then shattered, by Mar-tin's courtship of Sarah. Not that they had ever limited themselves to each other. They did what they felt like doing, and sometimes it was business. Linda, a fiery in-your-face second generation Hungarian, was not about to take the announcement lying down.

"Always something different, is that it, Martin? Twice a day isn't enough for you? Well you can fuck yourself from now on, buddy, and fuck you for bringing me to this cowtown in the first place. You'll never get anywhere from here. Now you're just another hick in a hick town, and you can screw the boss's daughter ten times a day and snort all the coke in California and it won't change that one bit." Two days later she left for Los Angeles. A ranch hand regular at the Sundowner drove her to her aunt's home in Culver City, and was allowed to spend the night with her there for his trouble.

* * * *

"Ernie, I'm devastated!" Sarah cried, when Ernie told her he was going to leave. "You're my partner. you're more than my partner. You're the engine here and I'm the caboose."

"Hardly, Sarah. I don't think you've ever been a caboose. There are certainly good people who'd be excited to come aboard here. You've got a loyal readership and a clear vision for what you want *The Echo* to become. I know you can make it happen. I'll help you find people if you want me to."

Truly shaken, Sarah looked down at her desk, around the office, out to the oak trees by the street. Her fists were clenched, and she held them tightly between her knees.

Finally she found words for what she wanted to say. "This vision for *The Echo,* Ernie, it isn't just mine. It's ours. Daddy's and yours and mine. You and I have given it a life, and dear God in heaven, I don't want it to be stillborn. If it's going to happen, Ernie, it will happen because we'll be doing it together. Please think about it. Please don't give me a 'no.'"

She's one powerful lady, Ernie thought. "Can anybody say 'no' to you, Sarah? You always know what you want and you always get it. That's a wonderful thing. I don't always get what I want, and that's probably my own fault. But I've got a lot to look at here."

"What is it, Ernie? Can't you tell me? I'll do everything I can to help you get what you want." She was leaning close to him now, looking directly into his eyes, and he thought she might just as well have kicked him in the stomach.

"If only. That might be beyond even you now, Sarah. All I can say is that some personal things have come up. You've got plenty of personal things too, a wedding to plan on top of everything with the paper. I'll tell you one way or the other in the morning."

At 3:00 a.m. Ernie got out of bed, dressed and began walking through Oak Hills' deserted streets. He had slept not a moment, his mind in turmoil. For this incredible, now unreachable girl. he felt a love he had never known, a connection with another person that was not just hormonal, but emotional, spiritual even. Now he knew she was the person he wanted to spend all the rest of his days and nights with and never would. It was the bitterest moment he had ever experienced.

For the first time, Ernest Hemmingway, at 32, was confronting himself. He had never taken charge of his life, what he wanted, where he was going. Everything had come easily. He was good. He had talent and had ridden on its wave. Many he knew didn't have half his ability, but seemed to be doing important things, really important, like choosing their life partners. Their families were their glory. Too easy, that was his story. Easy? Good? Hell and damnation, what's the use of being good at something if you never grab hold of what you really want? And then you lose it. There was a streetlight on the corner by the fire station and Ernie was standing right under it. He couldn't see his own shadow. I'm not really here! Then suddenly he knew what he would do. The realization made him smile, if only a little. Ernie, from now on you're the only one in charge of your life. You decide where you want to go, what you want to do, who you want to be with.

Sarah wept when he told her his decision.

"Ernie, I didn't sleep all night. I knew you were important to the paper. But until now I guess I never realized how much I needed you."

A week later, Ernie took pictures at the reception the Cardenas family gave in their beautiful courtyard. Nearly a hundred guests had been at the wedding. Sarah's brother had asked Martin weeks earlier if some of his family would be coming. "There aren't any," he'd answered. "I'm the end of the line." Vows were exchanged under the rustic wild rose archway that Sarah and Elena had run through countless times as children. George, Jr. stood as best man, Elena as maid of honor. Ernie put together a full-page feature for the society section.

June is the classic wedding month, and there were at least a dozen honeymoon couples on Catalina Island along with Martin and Sarah. She could tell. It was as obvious as if they had an H on their foreheads. For one thing, they didn't come out of their rooms early in the morning. Honeymooners were wonderful, she reflected, Jackie Gleason notwithstanding. She and Martin walked around the harbor town of Avalon, poking into the shops, drinking coffee at the sidewalk cafes, and she felt like she was back in France. The Wrigley Mansion on the hill above the harbor must be visited, she decided. Martin wanted to rent one of the mini cars that were the island's principle means of transportation, but she said, naw, sissy, let's walk up there. He was winded when they arrived, and she hadn't even worked up a glow.

"This is the house that chewing gum built," Martin read from a tourist brochure, when he had finally caught his breath. "There's a lesson in economics for you, sweety-pie; five cent chewing gum, sold to everybody in the world a few million times, and the guy buys himself an island."

They took a bus tour, saw the buffalo roaming on the hills, the yachts sailing into the coves. On a glass bottomed boat they attended a ballet of golden Garibaldi swimming beneath them. One day they snorkeled there, danced with the colorful fish, and played chicken with a two-foot barracuda. They went to movies at the Casino, petted in the darkened theater, and on Saturday, when a big band was playing, danced until the place shut down.

I've died and gone to heaven, Sarah thought, lying in the early morning hours beside her new husband, who had finally gone to sleep. How does he do it? she wondered. Her lover in Paris was no match for Martin. But this relationship was more than physical gratification; for the first time in her life she had given herself up wholly to another human being. She felt emotions she had never known existed. Her love for her father had been deep, but nothing like this. This was soaring, like the red-tailed hawk riding a thermal above the hillside outside their room.

* * * *

Two months after the wedding, on a weekend when Martin was in L.A. at a conference, Ernie and Sarah had lunch at Martha's. Since his decision under the street light, Ernie was different. He had redefined his role in *The Echo*. He'd made the company's expansion his personal goal, to be accomplished for his own sake and no one else's. He was proud of the toughness he had developed, working every day with the love he had lost, accepting the challenge. Sarah valued his enthusiasm for the paper, but had little understanding of why it existed.

"So much is happening all at once now, Ernie," she said across the table. "Martin says the business managers' meetings in L.A. are really helpful, especially the workshops. They're designed for papers like ours that want to grow. This is his third trip to L.A. in six weeks."

"We'll need all the expertise we can get, Sarah. Nothing like having a business manager in the family."

They knew Martin was in Los Angeles. They did not know that in addition to the $500 he had in his pocket for conference and living expenses, there was another $500, listed in *The Echo's* records as an account adjustment for an order of printers ink.

By the fall of the year Ernie and Sarah had formalized their growth plan for the paper. Martin absented himself from most of the planning sessions, saying he needed the state of the art information offered at the L.A. conferences. On his third trip, less than 60 days after he had become a married man, he had driven to Culver City, where he'd tracked down Linda Demeter's aunt. On the fourth trip, he spent several hours in Linda's apartment, which overlooked an Encino golf course, a hundred yards from an estate once owned by John Wayne.

The day she made the choice to leave Oak Hills and Martin, Linda Demeter began putting her body to more productive use than keeping company with small town rubes. It was hardly an overnight decision. Several regulars at the Sundowner had paid her for services rendered after closing time, but not what she knew she would earn with a more upscale clientele. On her initial outing she met a film score composer in a North Hollywood bar, went to his hillside house for the night and took home $200. It was a pattern easy to repeat. At bars and clubs she learned to spot patrons with potential. She bought a round bed, like one she had seen in the new *Playboy*.

Two blocks from where Linda lived, a custom home was under construction. She noticed a tall young man loading tools in the back of a pickup truck that advertised finish carpentry. She thought a moment, stopped her car, and with the late sun behind her, walked toward him. The day was warm and her dress was thin. She quickly had his attention. Yes, Johnny Dell did some moonlighting. That was all he did, in fact, because he was an independent contractor. With a tilt of her head and a half smile, she told him what she needed: floor to ceiling mirrors on two of her bedroom walls, a movie screen, and a slide projector. Certainly. She needed it right away. Certainly. Six days later Dell dropped by to get her approval of the installation. On the coffee table a magazine lay open to its centerfold. In the bedroom she asked, "Do you think this will work?"

"Don't see why not."

"We'd better make sure," she said. She drew the curtains, flicked on the projector, and a picture of a woman appeared on the screen, her assets clearly an invitation. Every ten seconds a different photo appeared, each more explicit than the last. Then she personally showed him what she had in mind. An hour later, pronouncing the installation a success, she had arranged to barter the labor cost of the project for her services over the next two months. The vodka she served Mr. Dell would qualify as a business deduction.

Linda was startled to find Martin at her door one afternoon, and nearly slammed it in his face. He persisted in spite of her very blue protests until she relented. Well, she'd had a long history with this idiot. Besides, he had some money in his pocket now, and coke doesn't grow on trees.

* * * *

Sarah hadn't seen a movie since she moved to Oak Hills. Back in her hotel room after her run on the beach, she showered, changed, and took a taxi to Westwood, where Hitchcock's *To Catch a Thief* was having a record engagement at the Village Movie Theatre. She had done all she could toward the press purchase, and the flick would be a change of pace. The whole trip to L.A. was giving her a break, apart from the goosey moment of plunking down $124, 575 dollars for a printing press, more than she expected to earn in the next five years. The majority of the audience for the film were students from UCLA, which was just next door. Shades of Berkeley, she thought.

Relaxed by the movie, Sarah slept well. In the Century Hotel's very small coffee shop, she sat at one of the six tables and ate a breakfast of Coachella Valley grapefruit (seedy), a soft boiled egg (a little hard), and strong black coffee (just right). This was an exciting day. Today she had no feeling of tension. The negotiations were completed, and all that remained was for her to sign the closing papers. She looked forward to that, and had brought along the black Waterman pen her father always used when he wrote her letters. It would be nearly a month before the press would be delivered, allowing plenty of time to pour a specially reinforced concrete foundation for it.

Sarah realized she had stars in her eyes about the

prospect of owning that equipment. The paper would be able to handle the needs not only of small firms, but major ones as well. Ernie had come up with four nationally distributed specialty catalogues that would fit perfectly with the printing capacity *The Echo* would have. The company could make as much revenue with competitively priced job printing as it could in publishing the newspaper.

The press was a high speed web made in Recklinghausen in the British Zone of Germany. She wondered momentarily if the firm that made it had benefited from the Marshall Plan. It was just before 9:30 when she set out for the Frawley offices.

There'll be lots to do this month, Madam Publisher. I just hope Martin gets back on the team. We really need his know-how. With new ground to cover in the county now, Ernie thinks we should buy a couple of surplus Jeeps for the reporters. I know they're cheap. But there's sure nothing cheap about Martin's car. Maybe if he drove a banged up Jeep he'd be less of a honey pot for harpies like that Haggarty. I still don't understand what happened there. Just asking him about her led to an almighty blowup . . .

Sarah had been startled when Martin purchased a two year old convertible from the Ford dealer in Tigh Harbor. He'd even had sheepskin seat covers installed, insisting that the car was good for the company. "It gives us an uptown image, as if Oak Hills has an uptown."

"Oh, c'mon, Martin. Just because we're not L.A. or 'Frisco doesn't mean there aren't a lot of classy people here. Anyhow, with this expansion we're going to put Oak Hills on the map in a way it's never been. And hey, how about both of us going to L.A. for the seminar next weekend? I'd really like to meet some of the people from those other publications. Their objectives sound a lot like ours, and I bet we'd have plenty to talk about. We might even take in a show at the Music Center!"

"Now that's a great idea. Or it would be if there were editors or publishers due to come for this one. Trouble is, they're all going to be bean counters, and I know how much you love bean counters. You'd stay awake about 30 minutes. And the evening workshops just go on and on. But I'll see when there's a seminar the mucky-mucks will be showing up for, and then you should come."

Sarah had been frustrated more than once by Martin's inaccessibility when he was at the seminars. Sometimes calls to his hotel weren't returned until the next day, because "a workshop ran late," or "everyone had gone out for dinner after the meeting and he didn't want to call back in the middle of the night." Then, last Saturday morning when she was at her beauty shop, her head tipped back in a sink for a rinse, two women at the back of the small salon were gossiping. One said she had been in Tigh Harbor the week before.

"And would you believe, I saw Martin Daniels at White Sands restaurant with that Haggarty woman."

"You didn't!"

"I most certainly did."

"The one who practically brags about sleeping with a different man every night?"

"That's the one. He had his arm around her waist, Tight-like, too. now what do you suppose is going on?"

Shaken and trying hard not to believe what she was hearing, Sarah wrapped a towel around her head and left the salon sopping wet. Her hairdresser had also overheard the gossiping women, and helped her leave unnoticed.

Who in hell is this Haggarty woman? And those meetings in Los Angeles! Always out late. God in heaven, it can't be. Can it? What have I been thinking? In a daze, she drove to the house. Martin was polishing his bright new convertible, admiring reflections of the cottonwoods in the highly waxed finish. She unwrapped the towel and shook her head, sending a few drops of water onto the hood.

"Hey, sweetie, you trying to wreck my wax job?"

"Maybe. Martin, who is this Haggarty woman in Tigh Harbor?"

"Haggarty? Haggarty?" He looked thoughtful. "Beats me."

"How does it beat you, Martin? So you didn't have lunch in the most expensive restaurant in Tigh Harbor last week with a woman named Haggarty?"

"Sarah, I haven't even been to Tigh Harbor for months except to pass through. Oh, Mrs. Westmoreland? That who you mean? I don't know, maybe her name was Haggarty once. I know she was divorced. Oh, yeah, I was getting gas on my way to L.A. a couple weeks ago and bumped into her at the service station. She's a rep for Consolidated Paper. She was telling me about a new web grade they'd developed that we might be interested in so we had a cup of coffee to talk about it. Why?"

"Well, why didn't you tell me about it, Martin? You used to keep me up to date. I want to know about those things."

"Okay, okay, I'll get you the specs she gave me. No need to blow a gasket. Jesus, you'd think it wasn't being handled or something."

"Martin, I frankly don't know what's being handled, or for that matter, who. We've been working our tails off to get this expansions set up, and I've got a feeling something's wrong. We can't afford to miss anything here."

"Miss anything? Jesus Christ, woman. What's missing is everything! This is a paper that hasn't gone anywhere since your father died and isn't ever gonna go anywhere ever again. Not in this cow-town."

"What? Martin, what are you saying? Why are you being like this? We've got to be a team to pull off this expansion. Our future depends on it, you know that. And another thing—those meetings in L.A. Why are you always so damned unreachable there? Have you got a salesgirl you've gotta have coffee with there too? Half the night? All night?"

"Goddam it woman, you don't know shit about what it takes to run the financial side of a business. There's a lot more to it than you have any idea."

"Well I certainly know it doesn't take an expensive convertible to make it run. Martin, that car is the most irresponsible purchase I can think of for us right now."

"Who said anything about us? This is my car. It's in my name. I bought it with my money."

"Money? What money? You never told me you had that kind of money."

"Yeah? Well lets make a list of things you didn't tell me, Sarah. You want to start with fuckin' Ernie?"

"Martin! Damn you. How dare you!

Sarah stormed back to her car in a rage, then drove recklessly to the office, totally ignoring speed limits, and scarcely aware of even driving there until she arrived. She barged through the door. Ernie was at his desk, and looked up with a quizzical expression.

"Hey, madam publisher. Been to church, I see."

Sarah's hair was wild, her face flushed, her blouse disheveled. "Come sit over her, young lady. Let me get you something to drink. And then maybe you'd like to tell me what's going on."

101

She sat in the chair by his desk, and neither said anything. Ernie went to the refrigerator and brought back two Cokes. At first, regretfully, but then with relief, she told him of her fight with Martin, her suspicions about the seminars in L.A., about the gossip she had overheard. "I don't really know anything for a fact, Ernie, but from the little I do know, it can't be good."

"No it can't. That's got to be miserable for you."

"Miserable is right . . . But there's clearly no future in being a victim. I'm not going to let this stop the world. If Martin opts out, that's his choice. You and I have been putting this together anyway. You know they confirmed this week that the Vegas press is available. I have first option on it until Wednesday, Ernie, and I'm going to take it."

"Good! That's the big plunge, Sarah. Scary maybe, but it's the sort of equipment that can give *The Echo* job printing capacity to generate some real income."

Encouraged and calmed by Ernie's support, Sarah sketched out her plan. She would leave in the morning, on Monday be at the L.A. offices of Frawley Cascade, the publishing chain that owns the press, sign the contract on Tuesday, then return via Las Vegas, where she would see the equipment and meet with the press room supervisor. Thanks to the success of the casinos and the growth of the city, the paper, a thriving daily, had outgrown its equipment and needed to triple its printing capacitiy. The capital fund her father had created would guarantee that she would get excellent terms for the purchase. Her father had sacrificed and overworked to develop the fund, and this was what it was created for.

"Ernie, I don't know what's going on with Martin, except that he's not supportive. When we started out the three of us had all those meetings about expanding. Now Martin says we should stay like we are. 'Nobody wants *The Echo* to change,' he says. He doesn't believe we can grow or even should. So I'm buying this equipment as owner and publisher, period. It's my decision, not his. Whatever's going on with Martin, Ernie, I know what I want to do."

That night Martin came home at 2 a.m. Sarah turned and looked at him. Neither spoke. *It was my thirtieth birthday today. He doesn't remember. Maybe never even knew.* In the morning she was up and out of the house early. She left a note on Martin's desk at the office saying she had business out of town and would be gone until Friday. She picked up the spreadsheets, left a note for Ernie that she would call, got in her car and headed for Tigh Harbor and the airport.

PART FIVE

It was just two days since Sarah had left Oak Hills and taken the plane to Los Angeles. Two days that felt like a month. In the Century City high rise, she once again punched the elevator button for Frawley Cascade's floor.

Well, Madame Publisher, she thought, as the numbers above the door clicked higher and higher, we'll sign the contract today and be off and running. Her father's Waterman pen was ready. The door hissed open and there was Miss Expensive, her perfect self. A few minutes later Mr. Cold Fish rounded the corner. Today, however, he was Mr. Frozen Fish. In a block of ice.

"Please come to my office, Mrs. Daniels." There, without asking her to sit, he said, "Mrs. Daniels, I don't know what you're expecting here, but neither of your accounts hold what you claim. Your 92283775 account holds just $4,226 and you claim $150,000 plus. Your 92283777 account holds $645 and you claim $8,684. Your D&B is less than 30 days old, and it's within 2% of those amounts. Therefore your option for purchase of this equipment is withdrawn."

"But that's impossible!"

"Mrs. Daniels, it is withdrawn."

"But I mean the accounts! There's a mistake. Something's wrong!"

"Yes, Mrs. Daniels, I agree. Something's very wrong. But it's not the numbers."

"But I brought you the spreadsheets just yesterday, and they're current!"

"Then they're current for a different business, not for yours. The receptionist will validate your parking."

It was the end of the world.

A Bank of America office was less than a block from the high-rise. Breathlessly, Sarah asked for the manager, explaining in a voice she knew was trembling that she was the publisher of *The Echo* in Oak Hills and in the middle of a very large purchase agreement and urgently needed to have copies of the paper's accounts. The woman was sympathetic and said she would do what she could to help. She called the Oak Hills branch, and learned there that the only persons authorized to access the account were George Baker and Martin Daniels.

Stunned, Sarah headed for the airport, where she canceled her ticket to Las Vegas. She barely caught the one daily flight to Tigh Harbor and sat on the plane in a daze, physically reeling from the blow she had received. Self recrimination, anger, fear, came in waves.

Damn, damn, damn. This just can't be! I've been back here for two years and I'm the publisher of this damn damn paper and I'm not even authorized to access its accounts. How is that possible? Because Martin never put you on the list, that's why. You just assumed everything was going along like it was supposed to. What an idiot! Daddy's still listed and he died two years ago. It's insane! No, you're insane, Sarah. Talk about not being responsible! Good lord, what will I find when I get in there?

Martin had said her father paid himself by automatic transfer to his personal account. He'd set the same thing up for Sarah, too, who took everything for granted because Martin was handling it and the business was doing so well! *Oh my God. Naive, stupid, damn! I trusted him! Because Daddy trusted him. Oh my God, was everything with Martin just a sham? Just to get his hands on the money? My God, it just can't be!*

But apparently it was. She got to the bank in Oak Hills shortly before closing time. It was one of BofA's smaller branches, and still had a folksy atmosphere, including the informality of the transactions. The manager, Francesco Cardenas, was Elena's cousin. Fourteen years earlier he had not too innocently skinny dipped with Elena and Sarah in the irrigation tanks at Papa Beto's fields. He was a graduate of Cal Poly San Luis Obispo, and had become manager of the branch just before George Baker had his heart attack. Yes, of course he would help. Your family is practically our family, Sarah. And yes, it was true, her father's name was still listed on the account, as was Martin's. But not Sarah's. But there was a notation to see documents on file. Cardenas looked them up.

They were two 1954 memorandums from her father, written in longhand. The first was dated the day she told him she would come back to Oak Hills. He wrote that she would become *The Echo's* publisher in approximately sixty days, and should then be placed on the accounts. The second was date stamped two days before her father died. It stated that until Sarah became publisher, Martin Daniels could disburse payments and conduct necessary business for *The Echo* without the authorization of a second signature. A copy of the memo had been sent to Martin. Both memos had been sitting in the file, unflagged and unnoticed for two years.

Then came the awful truth. The balances in the accounts were exactly what she had heard from Frawley Cascade. The capital improvement fund, a money market account, instead of the $150,000 she had been told was there, contained $4,649.32. The account history? Monthly transfers of $5,000 to $15,000 had been made to *The Echo's* operating account for more than a year. Cash withdrawals from the operating account had begun the same month she had first slept with Martin in the apartment above the paper. *That dirty, dirty bastard! He wasn't just fucking me. He was screwing me.*

Cardenas locked the bank when he left with Sarah. "I'll do whatever I can," he told her. "I've put a freeze on the accounts, and you should get a court order right away in the morning to slap an injunction on him. I'm not a lawyer, but even if he's your husband, this looks to me like embezzlement. It's not my place to ask, Sarah, but what in hell has he been doing with all that money?"

"I can't tell you yet, Francesco, but I'm certainly going to find out."

She drove toward her house slowly now, uncertain of what path to take, but icily determined to regain control. What would be served by yelling and screaming all by herself at Martin? She would do that when she had a lawyer and a cop with a pair of handcuffs with her. What were her options? Did she have anything left? The house, barn and all, wouldn't bring more than $15,000 if sold, and then where would she live? Upstairs at the paper?

The paper! Was there a viable paper left? My God, she'd have to get a lawyer to look at everything.

Sarah turned into the bottom of the lane to the house, and for no reason except to collect her thoughts, stopped the car. The day had been warm and her window was open. She heard music from the house, and lights were on. So Martin hadn't expected her and thrown a party! She opened her door and stepped onto the lane, a pathway she had always loved that now looked like the road to hell.

She closed the door and quietly walked toward the house, below the windows that overlooked the fields, now washed in violet by the afterglow of sunset. She heard voices, a woman's, more than one. They came from her bedroom at the north side of the house. Almost in a trance, she followed where the road ran beneath her window and the trellis covered by a blooming mass of pink wild roses.

Through the exotic framework the lighted room showed as clearly as a movie screen. It was an image Sarah would wish she'd never seen. On their bed, her bed, two women and her husband were sinuously entwined. She didn't linger to learn who was doing what to whom, but turned and walked to the front of the house. Martin's car was there, its top down. Parked close beside it was another convertible, a green Jaguar. She walked to the barn, found a shovel and two buckets, and filled them to the brim with still-steaming manure from the trough behind the cows. Robot-like, she carried them to the cars and dumped one onto the sheepskin covers of Martin's car, the other onto the leather seats and carpeting of the Jaguar. "Shit, shit, shit!" she cried in rage. Then she walked back to her car.

A quarter mile past the Cardenas house she pulled to the side of the road, aware that it was dangerous to keep driving. She was sobbing like a child. Every thought, every image that whirled through her mind made the hurt worse. She had opened her heart for the first time in her life, and it had been spit on, trampled on with jack boots. How sudden the slide from the best moments she could have dreamed of to the worst she could have feared. Half an hour later she realized she couldn't just keep sitting there. She could think of only one place to go, only one person she wanted to see.

But Ernie wasn't at *The Echo*. His car was missing, and a station wagon was in its place.

"Sarah Baker, did you just stick you finger in a light socket?"

The voice belonged to Kathy Stroud, her roommate and best friend in college, and Sarah would have recognized it in her sleep. "I've showed up unannounced this evening and then learned from the gal here you were in L.A. or somewhere. But here you are!"

"Yeah, Katie, I had a little detour. Oh, Jesus, what a detour. I'll tell you; you always find out everything in the first five minutes anyway. And by the way, it's Sarah Daniels, remember? I think."

"That bad, huh?" Sarah felt a kinship with Kathy as deep as her kinship with Elena Cardenas, and in some ways deeper. She had shared the secrets of her college days with this girl. With Elena the secrets were mostly about the naive, idealistic imaginings of youth. With Kathy they were grown up secrets, confessional quality stuff.

"Sare,' you need a drink, and maybe even some supper." Kathy put her arm around Sarah's shoulder and bundled her to her station wagon, a forest green Pontiac with *Sunset Magazine* and Lane Publishing emblazoned on the sides and the tailgate.

"Oh, you've graduated to the garden column, have you?" Sarah tossed out, trying for a little normality.

"You might say that, except that this is one very grown up garden. Lane has *Sunset Magazine,* and that's a big-

111

gie, believe me. But they publish lots of other stuff, and I'm doing a major book."

They drove to the south edge of town, where the road to Tigh Harbor leaves the city limits. The Golden Pheasant restaurant was there, as it had been for 35 years, surrounded by a minor forest of oaks and cottonwoods. The gin and tonic helped, especially the second one, and soon Sarah had told Kathy everything.

In their senior year at college they'd had more fun than you were supposed to have when you're getting a serious education. Since graduation, they'd met at least once a year somewhere, except when Sarah was in Paris. Kathy had made sure she heard every detail of Sarah's foreign affair, and had reciprocated with several of her own. She'd married eventually, and now had been divorced for 15 months.

"Martin sounds like a prick, if you'll pardon my French. Or Polish. Good grief, Sarah, and now you're telling me Ernie Hemmingway is working for you? Right here in Oak Hills? Well, it figures. I might have guessed."

"And what do you mean by that? Dad hired him and I had nothing to do with it."

"Listen, cutie, I went out with Ernie a couple of times, and while it distresses me to tell you this, he always seemed more interested in finding out about you than in making out with me. And it really distressed me at the time, believe me, because I thought he was a hell of a sweet guy."

Sarah sat stunned. When she felt tears coming she turned to the window, and saw only the lights reflected in the leaded glass.

Finally she turned back. "Well, if I could be that dumb about Martin, I guess I could be that dumb about Ernie. He's been my soulmate ever since I took on *The Echo*. For months we've been working on growth plans together. God, Kathy, I know Ernie a hundred times better than Martin, except for the sex. Right now I like him about a thousand times better. I've been able to count on Ernie since the beginning. Martin's all over the place. All those mood swings."

She looked hard at her friend, enough to make Sarah say, "What?"

"Coke, honey. Think about it. The car, the unpredictability. He sounds like a mirror image of the art director I worked with before Lane. Except he's not queer. I guess."

"Coke? My God! It never entered my mind." She sat astounded.

For the next fifteen minutes they talked about the signs and signals of addiction. She realized there had been more than a few. But Kathy's book was the official reason for her visit to Oak Hills.

"It's a coffee table production about some of California's family dynasties. The damn thing could be as big as Encyclopedia Britannia. You can't believe the editing that's going to be involved. It'll have the Huntingtons, Chandlers, Crockers, Hearsts, Irvines, Stanfords, and a few other luminaries. But I came today to pick your brain, such as it is, about Kenneth Caulfield."

"Kathy! Don't tell me you're putting him in the same category! He was no kind of a luminary, except in his own mind."

"Well, yes and no, kid. I know what he did to your dad was pretty shitty, but the fact is that Caulfield built a big business. Yes, he sold his editorial integrity. But he was just a little ahead of his time in that department; these days there's PR crap in lots of papers, and as far as magazines go, half the books in the country slip in references to their advertisers. They're quite up front about it. But your dad had a higher standard and wouldn't prostitute it; he got stomped on in the rush to the sellout."

"How come you're so eloquent on all this, Kathy? Been taking night courses or something?"

"No, girl, I've had it with school. My education began when I came to Lane. It wasn't that I had to unlearn college stuff. I just had to reprioritize it, learn about dealing with people, about publication politics and economics. That's why Caulfield is in the book."

"How so?"

"Well first, because he built a publishing empire, and don't make that face, damn it, you know he did. The Caulfield papers dominate the county. You've got advertising and circulation competition from them right here in Oak Hills. Second, including him will increase sales of the book in this part of the world. It's just publishing economics, Sarah. Third, the more 'luminaries' are in the book, the more the light shines back on Lane."

"Lordy, Kathy, Machiavelli never said it so good."

"That's show business, kid. Now, here's a teaser question: What happened to Timothy? It's a missing chapter in the Caulfield story. I spent part of last week in Tigh Harbor, talking with a lot of people, and on Saturday I went up to the cemetery to garner some history from the headstones. The big surprise was that Timothy Caulfield was there."

"That's what you told me on the phone, Kathy. It was a fantastic bit of news for us. Timmy grew up with my brother, dropped out of sight after high school, and nobody's heard of him for years. Dad always wondered if he might have been connected with the Ketterman murder because he just vanished after that. I don't know if it's because Timmy disappeared, but Georgie seemed different in some ways, too. He ought to know what you've learned. Where has Timmy been?"

"I have no idea, but I know where he is now, and it's nowhere you'd want to be"

For the next sixty minutes the two shared all they knew about the Caulfields. They had different reasons for wanting the information.

"I was puzzled that I could find out so little about Timothy," Kathy said. "Nobody could tell me where he went after he got out of school. And Caulfield's autobiography was just a dead end. There's a family picture in it where he's surrounded by his kids and grandkids, except for Timothy, with a footnote, (*son Timothy not in photo*). The kid would have been 29 when that picture was taken. When I saw the gravestone, I went back to check the morgue at the *Patriot* and there wasn't a word about a burial for Timothy, or anything written about him ever. There were dozens of mentions over the years about other Caulfields. Of course it was their own paper, but that family had a big presence in Tigh Harbor, and it was strange that Tim hadn't been mentioned somewhere. Hey, by the way, did you know Caulfield was a Senator?"

"Sure, Kathy, for eight weeks. It was a payoff from a lame duck governor after a senator conveniently retired just before the end of his term. Evidently Congress wasn't even in session, but Caulfield could still travel to Washington, hobnob with the President, fill up his pork barrel and return home a hero. He wanted to be addressed as Senator forever after."

"He's obviously your favorite pin-up boy."

"Well dammit, Kathy, he wrecked my father's life, and Daddy never got over the pain the whole thing caused to

mother. I've always known there were Caulfield skele-
tons somewhere. This one's got a headstone."

They got back to *The Echo* close to midnight and Ernie
was there. He had seen Kathy's car and been filled with
concern. Before he could say anything Sarah cried in his
arms. Kathy watched them briefly, then drove away.
Ernie said, "Let's walk a little." She told him everything,
including what Kathy had said about their college days.

"Damn you Ernie Hemmingway," she exclaimed, after
an hour wandering together along the darkened streets of
the town. "You could have had me up and down at
Berkeley. I was too proud to start things, but I knew I had
a heart connection with you that moved me. And damn
you, damn you, here I am blubbering all over you on a
bounce from my double-crossing two-timing good-for-
nothing—what I mean is, damn you, I want you in my
life—and I guess I knew it all along."

His eyes betrayed him. "Is that a proposal?"

She looked at him, could just see the outline of his face
in the glow from a porch light.

"Yes, damn you."

"I accept. It's the first time I've ever been proposed to
by a profane married woman. Or anybody, actually."

They stood there for awhile, and the reality of the moment, at least to a degree, began to saturate them. It was
an embrace they would long remember. Then they

walked to the Little Acorn Diner, Oak Hill's only 24 hour eatery. They emptied a whole pot of coffee and talked. Yes, Ernie had delivered to Martin an envelope from her father the day before he died. And yes, he'd mailed a letter to the bank. It seemed clear that Martin deliberately kept Baker's instructions from Sarah, and the bank had overlooked them.

"They could be sued for that, Ernie, but God, it's the Bank of America and they've got a million lawyers." She would need an attorney in any case, and told Ernie she would call Will Carlson in the morning, get an injunction against Martin, get him out of the paper's business and file for divorce.

"And one day maybe even make me legal. That's comforting," Ernie added wryly. But the hard part of the revelations was over. Now it was time to put their lives back together and plot a course.

∗   ∗   ∗   ∗

Much earlier that evening, in the ranch house bedroom, Martin had suddenly been assailed by the stench of fresh manure. He blanched when he discovered the cars. With both doors open, he sprayed the seats and floorboards with a garden hose. The big chunks were removable, but not the smell. Finally he went to the kitchen, got a knife, cut away the sheepskins and threw them sopping onto the ground.

"It's your wife," said one of the girls, grimacing at the disaster that used to be her beautiful Jaguar.

"Who else?" Martin returned. Two hours later, after he'd dried the cars as best he could with towels and blankets and sprayed them with Lysol, Martin left the house with two suitcases of clothing and personal effects. The girls left earlier, driving to their apartment in Tigh Harbor after Martin had promised he would pay to have their car professionally cleaned and detailed. They had agreed to have him stay at their place later that night. After all, they had reasoned, he has ten grand in his pocket, and "that smells a hell of a lot better than this fucking shitty car."

* * * *

Digging into *The Echo's* fiscal status with Ernie over the next few days, Sarah learned how disastrously deep was the pit into which she had been thrown. Her entire net worth could not begin to finance the expansion that had been her father's dream.

She stared at the resume she'd found in her father's desk. Martin had come with credentials. But how could I have been so stupid, so blind to who he really is? She had gone along with Martin that exotic night a year ago because she wanted relief from tension, and he had given it. But how had she ended up with a ring on her finger and an empty bank account?

"Can I ever trust my judgment again?" she asked Ernie, hating to admit self doubt.

"Sure," he replied, "providing you don't make too many profane married woman proposals." Partly to help restore Sarah's confidence and partly because he absolutely needed to know, Ernie put in a call to Angelo Cox, Chief Financial Officer of Doctors Hospital in Wichita, who was listed on Martin's resume as a reference.

The receptionist there referred him to the hospital's human resources director. "May I inquire what this is in reference to, Mr. Hemmingway?" asked the director.

"Well, to be frank, we've had some trouble with a person who was recommended to us by Mr. Cox."

"Mr. Hemmingway, I'm sorry to hear that. But I can only tell you that Mr. Cox is no longer with the hospital."

"Oh, did he leave recently?"

"I'm sorry, but I'm not at liberty to comment on that, on the advice of our attorneys."

Now Ernie's curiosity was thoroughly piqued. To his surprise, he found Angelo Cox through directory information, and Cox answered the phone himself. They talked for thirty minutes.

"Sarah, your father couldn't have known, and probably you couldn't have either. But you were dealing with a real crook and sleazebag. Cox told me that he is personally under indictment for embezzlement, and cooperating with the D.A. in hopes of getting a lesser sentence. The guy's falling all over himself, confessing to anybody who calls up, I guess.

"The story is, he'd skimmed off nearly $200 thousand over a four year period from the hospital, and hired Martin to cook the books. He'd given him a good recommendation when the guy came out here because they were then still partners in crime. Martin had to get out of Kansas to avoid being served in a paternity suite."

"What? Oh no! Oh my God, Ernie, what else is there?"

"That's enough, Sarah. An audit at the hospital uncovered the scam. Cox thinks they won't come after Martin because he'd claim he didn't know the numbers he was given were phony. But who'd believe that? The other reference was the Better Business Bureau. They're still giving Martin a positive reference as a CPA, and don't even know he's moved. Bloody Business Bureau, I'd call it."

"Ernie, this is not what either of us expected. I didn't beg you to stand by me until I went broke. You've got no chains to me now."

"What chains, Sarah? I made a promise to your father and a promise to you. They were never chains. Not even contracts. They're stronger than that." He grinned slyly. "Besides, you've proposed. Or were you drunk?"

Sarah couldn't help smiling. She was amazed to learn that Ernie knew of Martin's philandering before she did. The owner of a French bottling firm had come to Califor-

nia to buy the Oak Hills water business that sold premium mineral waters from the natural springs on the east
edge of town, one of which was located on Papa Beto's
farm. The purchase was big local news.

Ernie had driven to Los Angeles to get the first interview and had photographed the gallic gentleman in the
lobby of the Bonaventure Hotel. When the film was developed he was startled to see in the background of one
shot a clear image of Martin entering an elevator with a
woman who was obviously not his sister. The paper's lab
tech had scarcely glanced at the picture. Ernie removed
that print from the file, but kept it.

"But why didn't you tell me?" Sarah lamented, clearly
hurt that he had known.

"Because I love you, Sarah. Obviously you would find
out, and there would be no way of avoiding the pain. But
I never wanted you to hear about it from me."

* * * *

Their options seemed few. They considered them carefully during the following week. The unthinkable was to
do nothing. They looked at the pros and cons and decided
to concentrate on the pros. What were their strengths?
Journalism, obviously, was high on the list. Kathy
Stroud's discovery of Timothy Caulfield's grave had

glittered for 48 hours as the first real lead in the mystery of Who Killed Ursula Ketterman? Then it had vanished from sight and mind beneath the landslide of slime and deceit from Martin. But the clue was still there!

"Who Killed Ursula Ketterman!" Sarah exclaimed suddenly. Clarity came with the brilliance of an exposé! An exposé it would be, in fact, with the pedestrian label of Investigative Journalism: the unsolved murder of Ursula Ketterman and the sudden disappearance of Timothy Caulfield that had haunted George Baker for more than a decade. Finding the connections, and the truth, would become their focus. "Who Killed Ursula Ketterman?" would be their "Blaze of Glory" investigation.

"And Ernie, if it's our final edition and *The Echo* comes off looking like a London tabloid, so be it."

Frank McGee

PART SIX

Sarah showed Ernie the gravesite. Again, the day was beautiful.

"Sarah, you said Kathy found no record in the *Patriot* of Timmy's burial? That's very strange, because he was family. That has to tell us something. At least the county clerk's office will have a notice of interment."

But it didn't. The girl at the desk said they only kept record of people who died in the county, so this person must have died elsewhere.

At the cemetery office the young man in charge was only too glad to tell them about the Caulfields' graveyard history. Evidently he didn't have many visitors doing historical research. The Caulfields have a beautiful site, and yes, Timothy was the most recent family member to come to us. The undertaker? Just a moment.

The records were all in order, as perfect as the carefully trimmed grass between the headstones. The mortuary address was in Pasadena, just north of L.A. Ernie and Sarah were both aware their stomachs were asking for lunch, so they picked up burgers at Bob's Big Boy drive-in and headed for the city. Ernie, driving Sarah's car, was careful not to spill pickles on the seat.

At the Pasadena address they'd been given, no mortuary existed. There was a small auto repair shop across the street. Its owner told them the mortuary had moved about six months earlier, along the same street four blocks to the west. Those four blocks led from the fringe of this commercial part of town to the start of a pleasant residential neighborhood. The new mortuary building was imposing, a two story red brick structure, with four white pillars soaring from the entrance level to the roofline. A much better image, Ernie thought.

Again, the young man in charge was happy to help. Yes, we've moved. We have new owners, and they felt this location would be more in keeping with the service we offer to the community. Old records? Of course. They're all right here. Again, perfectly ordered.

"We're inquiring about Timothy Caulfield."

"May I know what your interest is?" Kathy Stroud had prepared Sarah for the question.

"Oh certainly. We're doing a history of a number of leading California families, and learning where information might be found is, well, in some cases it's really rather a daunting task. Frankly, it's wonderful to meet a person who's as efficient as you evidently are. You may even have knowledge of what took this unfortunate man at such a young age."

"Yes, of course. It's right here in the death certificate."

"Oh. Does it indicate where he passed away?"

"Certainly. At Casa Encanta Hospital, on East Sierra Madre."

Casa Encanta was fifteen minutes away, enough minutes for a quick look at the Certificate of Death, which the accommodating gentleman at the mortuary had obligingly, and amazingly, mimeographed for them. Ernie was certain that had he visited the mortuary without Sarah, he would not have been given the document, or perhaps even shown it.

"He had bipolar disorder, it says here, Ernie. Ha! Doesn't everybody?"

"Well, historically it was called manic depression, and it could have been a kind of a catch-all diagnosis. Might mean chronic schizophrenia, isochronal delirium, repetitious paranoia, or something else."

"Goof Lord, did you study medicine too?

"No, just interested in stuff like that. When I was in college there was a big court case about a veteran who'd killed his wife. He claimed she'd been some kind of secret agent placed with him to learn military secrets. The poor gal had been his high school sweetheart, and waited three years for him during the war. The professor had us write essays about the case, and I read up on what might have been going on in the guy's mind. Never did figure it out."

"Oh my God."

"Well, I doubt the guy paid much attention to Him."

* * * *

Casa Encanta was set well back from the road, nearly hidden by gigantic oaks that had been growing for generations. Again, red brick, with sharply peaked roofs. An enormous lawn behind the building bestowed a golf course-like setting for the mix of trees, shrubs and flowers that would have done justice to a national arboretum. Casa Encanta, charming indeed. The hospital's brochure described the institution's purpose as "redefining mental health care," and wrote of hope and renewal. The records department offered little hope of information, however, only that Timothy was a resident from July, 1952, until his death in 1954. Where had he lived prior to coming to Casa Encanta? Sequoia.

Another piece that fit the puzzle. J. Kenneth Caulfield, Timmy's father, had died in 1952. His ranch, the JKC, was up on the mesa, the high country some 75 miles above Oak Hills. The nearest town with a grocery store was Little Sequoia. The only direct road to Little Sequoia from Oak Hills was respectfully called The Rattlesnake; it wound up the canyon above the sometimes violent, always tortuous Feather Rock River.

"I've been through that country," Ernie recalled, as they headed back to Tigh Harbor. "There's not a sequoia tree in sight."

"Timmy must have come from his father's ranch,"

Sarah said. "Georgie knew Timmy since they were kids, and they stayed friends even though Dad hated Kenneth Caulfield. Georgie told me once the kid usually needed encouragement, and for some reason, he was always willing to give it to him. But needing encouragement isn't exactly being bipolar. And Ernie, we've got nothing that connects Timmy with the murder of Ursula Ketterman. All we know is that's when he dropped out of sight."

In the archives of the Tigh Harbor Library they looked through yellowed, brittle newspapers from 1942, searching for Timothy clues. Headlines showed the thunderheads of war that loomed menacingly that year across a beautiful summer. Boys turning eighteen faced the draft. The call-up was announced. Pearl Harbor had changed everything.

At the end of August, Ursula Ketterman was murdered. She vanished on a Friday evening. Her mother said she had walked from their house to spend the night with an elderly friend who was unwell. "On an errand of mercy," the grieving mother had declared. They found Ursula's violated, beaten body on Sunday morning in an obscure corner of a large unwalled estate. The *Patriot* reported the progress of the investigation, including interviews with J. Edmund Russell, the sheriff in charge of the case (his name was always printed with the J). J. Russell declared that all information, "no matter how fantastic," would be examined. The *Patriot's* stories emphasized the victim's religious devotion and exemplary character.

"Choir Girl Killed," headed the caption beneath a photo of the girl, distinctive only in its sameness with photos of other young women of the time.

The Echo, in Oak Hills, had printed a well researched profile of Ursula and her family. Her father had worked for years as a church and school janitor, and her mother did laundry for clients who could afford her, families such as the Kenneth Caulfields, the Jonathan Qualles (president of Keaton School), department store owner Herman Weil, and socialite Anita Allison. At some homes she stayed for the day, at others a few hours. The Kettermans had several older children. Ursula had been born after a barren decade.

The Echo's writer, Louis Els, a name neither Sarah nor Ernie recognized, had interviewed persons acquainted with the Ketterman family. In a few cases, he reported, he had been told conflicting stories, a comment that especially interested Ernie. Ursula belonged to the Daughters of Phythias, and while the organization's leader spoke kindly of the girl, it was in guarded, almost protective, terms. The writer received a similar impression from friends at her church, hearing words like "sweet," "dull," and once or twice, "simple." One young man, who wore thick reading glasses and said he had been in a class with Ursula in high school, described her as "slow."

"What do you mean by 'slow,'" the writer had asked. "Very, very slow," he answered. The most interesting information, however, came from families who employed her mother, Ruth Ann Ketterman. Ursula, it seems, was always with her. Apparently that had been the case since she graduated from high school. At the time of her death she was 20 years old, physically well developed, obviously capable of working.

Yet she was of little help to her mother, who not only allowed it, but apparently took it for granted. "Anything Ursula did had to be done over anyway," a neighbor had told Els. One of Ruth Ann's clients was the Roger Tillig family. Mr. Tillig had made the arrangements, although he was never at home when she had worked there. Mrs. Tillig had some kind of mental disorder, and had entered what the family referred to as her "second childhood." Their daughter, who had been 16 at the time of the murder, had been home on several of the family laundry days in the summers of '41 and '42.

"Ursula would play dolls with my mother all day long," the daughter stated. "At first I thought it was a nice thing for my mom, but it began to be really creepy. One day she brought a doll of her own to the house. 'This is Princess,' she said to me. 'Say hello to the lady, Princess.' I don't think the girl was normal."

Els had noted that various labels placed on Ursula Ketterman suggested she was 'different' than other young women. Not entirely different, he seemed to suggest, in the item with which he'd ended his article.

"In the well thumbed Bible by Ursula's bedside," Els wrote, "her mother found, in Ursula's hand on a small bit of paper:

    Roses are red

    And violets blu

    I will love you for always

    An angel told me to"

* * * *

The senior class at Keaton School graduated in June, 1942. Timothy Caulfield received his diploma in the spring ceremony, but had to attend summer school through July and most of August to graduate. He lived on campus in a ground floor room at the hillside home of Keaton's president, Jonathan Qualle. It was an extraordinary arrangement, Els had written, as the dormitories were closed and no other summer school students stayed on campus. Kenneth Caulfield had made the arrangement with Qualle, insisting the boy receive a diploma; without evening tutoring after the classes, he would fail. That, of course, would not be acceptable. (Els avoided the use of such "editorializing" language in his article, but the inference was there.)

Timothy Caulfield had long been a puzzle, at least to his father. His first wife gave him four unpuzzling children before she died, and he expected more of the same when he married again. First came a daughter, Tim's sister, who perfectly followed suit with her half siblings. But Timmy had a different gene. Nothing selfish, but nothing quick or sure. Childhood photographs showed an endearing boy, who radiated a sweet disposition. But he'd need more than that in the real world, his father knew, and giving him "more" was not as easy as closing a business deal, or getting a friend elected, or an opponent trashed.

Timmy tried hard, but was not a good student. Nor was he well coordinated. He could ride a horse, but rarely catch a ball, could walk for miles, but hardly run a hundred yards. Yet he was likable, and vulnerable. By the time he reached his teens, Timmy felt a desperate need to prove himself, project some kind of manliness, some strength. He entered Keaton School when he was fifteen.

Keaton students have access to one of the best sailing programs in the state. The school has a private beach, its own boat dock and a fleet of small racing sloops. Timmy found that sailing was something he could do, and do well. It was a victory of no small proportion. For the first time in his life he saw himself on par with the next guy; racing the Keaton sloops didn't require brute strength, just average strength, determination, and an understanding of airflow.

His older brother had sailed ever since he could remember, and owned an 8-foot sabot. There was a boathouse on the family beach, and the senior Caulfield's 22-foot Chris Craft runabout was housed there. A hand operated winch was used for launching, rolling the craft from the boathouse down two iron tracks into the water. When the tide was out, launching was easy, thanks to gravity. Putting the boat back was another story, best done when the tide was high. The Chris Craft as a result was seldom used, but the little sabot was easy to drag across the narrow beach to the water.

When Timmy was ten years old, he had picked up the art of sailing from his brother, fascinated with how the wind pulled the boat by lowering air pressure on the front of the sail. Although he found it almost impossible to study schoolwork at home, he avidly read sailing stories. In his first year at Keaton, Timmy not only made the sailing team, but won a single handed regatta.

The senior Caulfield was more than pleased by his youngest son's performance, so pleased that he bought him a sloop exactly like those owned by the school. When Timmy was home on weekends he could sail to his heart's content, and polish his skills in the process. Caulfield began rating the boy not so puzzling after all. He was not to know.

At 7:30 every Saturday morning, Ruth Ann Ketterman arrived at the Caulfield home to do the family's laundry. She stayed until it was nearly dark. She had seven children. Ursula, her youngest, was always with her. The girl had been a difficult birth, born when Ruth Ann was 47 years old. When Ursula was nine, her youngest sibling was already 20, the oldest 32. the Kettermans lived south of Tigh Harbor, across the Feather Rock River on county land. The area was not incorporated, but a town center had developed over the years, with retail stores, a bank, and a number of well-attended churches.

In time the community had become known as Feather Rock, and residents took pride in their collective closeness. The county board of education built a grammar school in Feather Rock in the twenties, and a high school in the thirties, to provide education for the families of the town and areas to the south and east. Tigh Harbor High School was in a separate district and served Tigh Harbor residents only; there was a tangible awareness of the class differences between the schools and communities.

Ursula Ketterman and Timmy Caulfield had no awareness of any such distinction. The ritual of the Saturday schedule had begun when they were toddlers. Typically they would spend hours at the water, building sandcastles, drawing pictures in the sand with sticks. "This is you, Timmy. Or maybe it's Clark Gable." Eventually, when Timmy had learned how, they sailed. The Ketterman mother came to appreciate her daughter's friendship with the Caulfield boy. He seemed guileless and innocent, and she was at ease with his guardianship of her youngest.

This could be considered mystifying, since her daughter was the older of the two, and two years is a major age difference for pre-teens. Yet the relationship proved convenient for both. Neither was outgoing by nature, for different reasons. When Timmy's mother remarked to her husband one day on the curious friendship, Caulfield told her it was probably good for the boy, and made no mention of differences in station.

* * * *

The secret life of Timothy Caulfield was far more visceral than his father realized. He'd been fourteen when he sailed the sabot with his First Mate, Ursula, around the point to the cove. It was early in the summer vacation. He'd visited the cove the year before with his brother, but Carter was hiking with friends in Yosemite, and this time would be Timmy's first adventure as Captain of the ship. In defiance of clear instructions from his father, he'd be out of sight of the family property. Carter was permitted to sail wherever he wanted to. Last year he'd skinny dipped in the cove. Timmy had to remain in the boat and sit on one side for balance when his brother climbed back in. The bluff above the cove was rimmed with wind-twisted cypress trees. Steep cliffs delineated the sides. The tiny bay was no more than sixty yards wide, an all but hidden crack in the weathered skin of the coast.

Ursula grinned with delight as they rounded the point, as usual comporting herself like a little girl, but today with the thrill of conspiracy. Timmy had told her before they started out that this was to be a secret mission,

136

something that no one would know about but themselves; the thought of intrigue excited her enormously. The fact is she had no secrets. Her emotional and social development was so slow from childhood that her mother had felt obliged to become her lifelong baby sitter.

In the tight knit community of Feather Rock, Ursula's teachers babysat her at school, carefully looking after "one of our own," helping move her from one grade to the next. She went to church, sang in the choir, remained a Daughter of Phythias, often cocooned by pity, protected from reality by the good intentions of others. The very thought of having a secret touched a hidden nerve in Ursula. She could know something, have something, that would be hers alone. Because it was naughty, it was even more exciting. "We won't tell anybody, will we Timmy? This is just our secret?"

The next Saturday they returned to the cove, earlier this time. Ursula told Timmy that her two sisters still living at home had no idea of their secret. "They didn't even ask what I'd been doing. But of course they never do. Mommy likes me to be with you."

"You want to know another secret?" Timmy asked her.

"Yes, I do!"

"But this is really secret. This is so secret if you tell you'll die!"

"Oh gosh, Timmy!"

"You promise?"

"Oh yes, I do. I'll never tell anybody ever."

"Last summer Carter went skinny dipping here."

"Skinny dipping?"

"Yeah, swimming without a bathing suit. He sat right where you are, took off all his clothes and dove in."

"Ooh," Ursula said, smiling a little at the picture that flashed into her mind. She was sixteen. She'd imagined pictures like that before.

The look on Ursula's face revealed to Timmy the image she saw, and possibilities it might present. He was at the age where such possibilities assumed enormous importance. The previous February he had discovered that the oak tree in the backyard at home offered the possibility of a view of his sister's bedroom window. There was a hill behind the tree, which screened the house from the neighboring property, and as a result his sister never pulled down her blinds. She was 18. Once Timmy had discovered the arbor vantage point, he used it whenever he could, one hand on the tree, the other in his pants. Once he came close to getting caught when his mother let the dog out into the yard, but his hormones were undeterred.

Now he looked at Ursula. She'd gone along with anything he wanted to do since he could remember. She wasn't like the girls at school, who made him feel like a little kid, not in the same class as guys who were cool. Ursula had always gone along with him.

"Do you want to?" he asked her.

"Want to what?"

"Go skinny dipping."

Ursula blushed visibly and lowered her eyes. When she looked up he could see there was a sparkle in them. At that moment they were floating in the bay with the sail furled. There was little wind.

"I'll go first," he said. "You have to stay in the boat to help me get back in, then you can go." He removed his sneakers, socks, shirt, and trousers, stowing them under the board where the mast was stepped. He wore only Jockey briefs, and when he looked at Ursula he saw she was wide eyed. He took off his briefs and quickly went over the side in a good imitation of a belly flop.

Now she was laughing. Timmy swam a few times around the boat, then grabbed the side and rocked it as if to tip it over. Ursula screamed in mock terror, still laughing. He knew she could swim. After a few minutes he turned on his back and floated, his feet pointed toward the stern where Ursula sat. She looked down at him, and in spite of the shriveling effect of the chilly water, he felt himself responding. She watched him, fascinated.

Getting back into the sabot was not as easy as he had expected. He was not as tall or strong as his brother, and it took him several tries. She helped him finally over the rail, getting herself soaked in the process. She was laughing when he reached up and kissed her. It was a little kiss as kisses go, but she stopped laughing and gasped.

He dressed then, and she told him she was getting cold, and they set sail for home. For a time neither said anything. When they were nearly at the beach, she said, "Can we go back?"

The next week they went again, and this time she swam. He showed her how she aroused him, and they touched each other and kissed, and brought their bodies together and held them, learning the feel of it. They made love in the boathouse, on a blue canvas boat cover beside the Chris Craft. It was the first time for both of them, awkward for him, painful for her. But it was never awkward or painful again, whenever Timmy could be home on Saturdays, and it was their secret. Parents, protective or sincere, are sometimes the last to know. When Timmy entered Keaton School and proved himself as a sailor, he was no longer restricted by his father as to where he was allowed to venture. They sometimes made love on the deck of the racing sloop, under the naked sky.

For nearly two months after Timmy's ceremonial graduation from Keaton at the acceptable age of 17, he never came home. His father had arranged for special on-campus tutoring: an hour and a half in the evenings and six hours on Saturdays and even Sundays. All of Kenneth Caulfield's children had gone to college, unerringly on track for advanced degrees. He was determined that his youngest son would possess his high school diploma. When Timmy was first given the ultimatum of this mandated academic effort, it seemed like the end of the world, but then he remembered there would be Fridays.

Summer school classes ended at four, at which time students who had cars headed for home, crisscrossing with the traffic of parents arriving to pick up their sons.

Friday was Mrs. Ketterman's work day at Keaton. She did laundry for the principal's family, and Ursula was with her, as always. Occasionally, when she was unable to finish her ironing before dark, Ruth Ann would allow Ursula to walk home by herself.

"I'll be just fine, mother. I know the way perfectly, and I'll turn all the lights on at home." The school was less than a mile from the Ketterman home, out the entrance gate, across the bridge, three blocks ahead, six blocks to the left, two to the right, 723 Pine Street.

The Keaton greenhouse was the only non class building on campus left unlocked during the summer session. At the rear of the greenhouse a partition separated a 15-foot space for supplies and equipment. The frosted glass on the roof had been painted white, to keep the area cool. A couple dozen bags of decorative bark were stacked along the end of the room. During summer school, shortly after four o'clock on every Friday, Ursula would be waiting for him there.

* * * *

The night of the June graduation, Timmy had been to a party at Randy Russo's. Randy's father owned a bank, Harbor Hills. His home was near the top of the highlands incline, a half mile below the cemetery, and it had a view of the coast from every west-facing room. There was a pool with curved sides, and a patio covered with multi colored Montana flagstone. Timmy had been there more than once. Randy had no brothers or sisters, and was on his third mother, that he could remember. His parents were away a good deal, at that particular moment in Maui, "hopefully getting back for your graduation."

He was christened Randolph, a name he had ditched at age five after he couldn't spell it on the first day of first grade, and the bossy girl next to him had snickered. Randy and Timmy connected at Keaton. It was months before they discovered why, and of course neither ever admitted it. Both were lost. Randy felt like an orphan, a rich kid orphan without real parents. Timmy felt like a loser, desperate for friendship, despairing of ever measuring up. Randy had been with any number of girls, owned a green 1940 Ford coupe, and knew how to use money to get what he wanted. He liked to go into detail about his conquests, and Timmy listened, bursting at times to affirm his own prowess, but always keeping his secret. He was either too shy, too loyal, too embarrassed, or too cowardly. Yet each gave the other something he lacked: acceptance.

"We'll celebrate getting out of this shit hole," Randy

had said at lunch time two days before the graduation party, his mouth stuffed full of institutional lasagna. "Half the class are comin'. There's buckets of booze in the house, and I got a guy comin' over with a projector and a really dirty movie. Why not go off with a bang, if you catch my drift. Ha!" He laughed at his cleverness. Timmy got permission from his mother to stay the night at the Russo's, conveniently leaving out the information that both parents were out of town.

At the party, everyone drank themselves close to oblivion. Inhibitions, whatever they might have been on a good day, were less and less in evidence as the evening progressed, or regressed. The movies, one filmed in Paris before the war, and a new one in a Southern California setting, were erotic, and the graduating seniors made ribald sport of trying to top each other with claims of their own exploits. Timothy Caulfield, as usual, felt diminished before the boasts of the school's athletes, debaters and extroverts. It was 3:00 a.m. before the last revelers headed down the hill, hopefully to reach home in one piece. The patio beside the pool looked like a Movietone News movie of a war zone.

"Lets clean it up in the morning," Randy groaned. He stripped off his clothes and flopped in the pool. Timmy, full or rum and Coke and barely able to stand, followed suite. The water jolted him from his stupor somewhat, and when they climbed out he said to Randy, "Hey, I screw all the time."

143

"Yeah, sure you do, jerkoff, with a banana peel."

"Naw, jeez, I mean it, Randy, I do all the time. Every Saturday."

"What the hell you talking about, Caulfield? You don't fuck nobody."

"Honest. Saturdays. This afternoon."

"What? C'mon. Whatcha talkin' about? With who?"

"Well," Timmy said, so drunk he could scarcely hear the alarm bells in his head, "with Ursula."

"Who? What? Ursula? Ursula Ketterman? No shit!"

"No shit."

"I don't believe you."

"Well, I do."

"Hell you do."

"Okay, I'll show you."

They stumbled into the empty house, flopped down on the living room carpet, and went to sleep. In the morning, head splitting and stomach retching, Timothy reluctantly reaffirmed to an insistent Randy that he would keep his word. "I'll have to figure out how though, but I'll show you. Oh, God, I'm sick."

Summer school began the following Tuesday. On Friday, Timmy and Ursula had their first summertime rendezvous in the greenhouse. They'd arranged it on the two

Saturdays before graduation, when it became apparent that Timmy would be doing indentured academic service at Keaton during the holidays, and not coming home on weekends. Ursula was jumpy with the prospect of the assignation at the school, but the fact that her mother never insisted she help with the laundry work meant that she spent a great deal of time out of her mother's sight. Ruth Ann Ketterman evidently felt her daughter was safer accompanying her to her clients than she would have been at home in an empty house, where she might have injured herself or wandered off. In Ursula's mind, going with her mother meant she'd have a different play-ground every day. She was 20 years old in body, but her mind was not at all difficult for Timothy Caulfield to ma-nipulate.

"Sweetheart." She smiled every time he called her that. and now as he whispered it his lips were against her ear. They were lying on the sacks of bark, not too bad, she thought, as long as they could be together. It had been as wonderful as always, and she wrapped her legs around his and hugged him to her.

"Somebody loves you," he whispered.

"I love you too, Timmy."

"Somebody else loves you."

She raised her hands and pushed him off her body. He was smiling. So everything was fine. It was important that everything was fine with Timmy. She loved him.

"But he doesn't think you could ever love me, like this, I mean."

"Oh but I do! And always will."

Timmy rolled onto his side and looked up at the frosted glass above them. "Honest? for always?" He seemed unsure.

"Yes, sweetheart, honest for always," she said, sitting up.

"Because he's supposed to be my friend but he's being really mean to me, and he says he'll keep on being mean until he knows for sure that we're doing, you know, this, the way it should be done, and that I'm giving you all the satisfaction you deserve."

"Oh but you are. This always feels so good."

"But how can he know?"

"Well, you could say something to him and then he'd know. Or would he tell his mommy?"

"He'd probably tell her unless he could see it for him-self. If he could do that, then he'd keep it secret. Like we do."

She saw the concern on Timmy's face. He was always carefree when they were together.

They'd been friends since she could remember. He'd always been so sweet, and then they had their secret, and looking forward to seeing him every week had become the emotional engine of her life. Nobody should be mean to Timmy, nobody should worry him.

"I suppose we could prove it to him," Timmy mumbled, "then it would be secret forever."

"Then he wouldn't be mean to you anymore?"

"No, he wouldn't. And because he loves you, he'd be happy that you're happy and he and I could go back to being friends again."

"That's good, sweetheart. He'll be happy and we'll be happy and we'll all have a secret." Timmy left the greenhouse and headed back to the classrooms, to come from that direction when he went to supper with the staff. Next week he'd prove to Randy he had what it takes. It would be the first time he'd ever been able to do that.

Ruth Ann Ketterman tried many times to put Ursula to work, but the girl's capacity for distraction was limitless and her work invariably needed redoing. She found it expedient to simply babysit her. She had done this now for years. To some who witnessed the connection only at a glance it seemed touching; a devoted daughter, fully grown, helping her mother with her work. But a closer look revealed a human pet, leashed by a cord that had never been cut.

This week was a roller coaster for Ursula. On Sunday she had sung in church, wearing her blue choir robe. Mommy had washed the robes for the church once, and the pastor had thanked her from the pulpit! When the congregation sang Leaning on the Everlasting arms, she thought of leaning on God's arms, and then a few flashes of leaning on the arms of Timmy Caulfield. Timmy had told her they had nothing to feel guilty about, and that God made people to enjoy each other like they did. She didn't listen to anything else in the service.

Monday was laundry day for the Kettners, where she played with their dogs and talked with their bird, but she'd felt afraid when she thought about Timmy's friend coming with him to the greenhouse. Tuesday was with the Tilligs, where she played dolls with the mother, and that made her happy. Wednesday was the Rafords; there she floated flower petals down the fountain that spilled into the pool (her mother always made her take them out before they went home). Thursday was with old Mr. Gifford in the morning and the Halustoks in the afternoon. It was kind of an up and down day, mostly just nervous about Friday.

Friday was the Badinskis in the morning, and Keaton School in the afternoon. She had never learned the name of the family, just Keaton School. Keaton was the only one of her mother's customers so close to her house that she could walk home on her own. It made her feel very independent.

Timmy and his friend came to the greenhouse right after 4:00 o'clock. She had a watch, with Mickey Mouse on the face, and his hands pointing to the numbers. It was Swiss, and she had received it on her 18th birthday from her uncle, her mother's brother, an engineer in Switzerland, "where everything had to be perfect." She looked at the watch every few minutes, just to see Mickey's hands move. She knew exactly where she was supposed to be at 4:00 o'clock this Friday. She got there early.

Ursula didn't look up when Timmy introduced Randy, although she could tell he was taller than Timmy, and darker. Timmy said some things she couldn't remember afterward, about how Randy was a really good friend, and that he really liked Ursula, and that he really wanted her to be happy and really satisfied like she deserved to be, something like that. It was different having another person there, and she didn't feel the same as when it was just Timmy and her. But Timmy said it would be alright and that Randy would just sit over there by the wheelbarrow and that when he was sure that she was really being satisfied like she should be he wouldn't be mean to Timmy any more and we would all have the secret together.

So Randy sat down and Timmy put his arms around her and hugged her, and moved his hands over her back and waist and up around her neck and the back of her head. After a little he moved down her back and then she started to feel more like she was supposed to and wanted to, and his hands on her chest made it more so even. Then they were up against the bags of chips, and he kind of scootched her up to sit on them and stood up against her. He moved her legs apart so he could stand closer, and had to push her skirt up some to be able to put his hand there, and she was feeling it a lot now, and she could see Randy over on the side, sitting watching them, smiling at her. It kind of made her flutter in a way she hadn't experienced before, and she sort of liked it.

Then Timmy was up on the sacks and lying on her and they were doing it. She was pretty near the explosion, as Timmy called it, when she looked over and saw that Randy wasn't sitting there anymore. She looked toward her feet and saw that he was standing there, close to her, and that he was showing himself to her. Timmy couldn't see him, but she could, and it just amazed her to see how different he was from Timmy, how much darker and wider and bigger, and how much more hair he had. Her eyes were wide open, looking, and then she shut them because she felt the explosion.

When she looked again, Randy was sitting back by the wheelbarrow, smiling a lot now. After a few moments, Timmy got off her and said something she didn't remember afterwards. But Randy said something about that being pretty good but there was one thing he wanted to make sure of, maybe next week. and she said to Timmy that it would be okay to bring Randy next week so they could be sure, and that's how the Fridays got started. The next week it was Timmy and then Randy, and the week after that Randy and then Timmy, and it switched back and forth and was both of them twice every Friday afternoon. Timmy's schoolwork didn't improve much during the summer, but probably didn't suffer either, and his academic incarceration wasn't nearly as distressing as he expected it would be.

The last day of summer school was Friday, August 28, and the attitude of students and teachers was festive, although some of the students still hadn't done well enough in their studies to graduate. Timothy Caulfield hadn't left the campus since the beginning of June. His mother would arrive to collect him at 6:00 o'clock. He'd have dinner at home for the first time since the beginning of the summer.

PART SEVEN

Ernie and Sarah read and re-read the newspaper accounts of the murder. The girl's body had been found a mile and a half up the Feather Rock River, on a seldom used trail through a eucalyptus grove on the estate of a famous orchestra conductor. His caretaker, out for an early walk on Sunday morning, had literally stumbled across her. Deputy Russell and officer Kirby had arrived at the scene almost at the same moment, responding to the police radio call about the gruesome discovery. It was clear how she had died. She'd been strangled with a cord or wire and her skull crushed with a blunt instrument. The autopsy report stated she'd been raped.

What had staggered everyone who knew Ursula even slightly, and had elicited vehement denials from her mother, was the coroner's statement that the girl was pregnant. When her mother heard this she had dropped to the floor in a faint. Later she vehemently denied it could have been true. Absolutely, totally impossible, she insisted. There were signs Ursula had struggled fiercely, and skin under her fingernails indicated she had scratched her attacker. Her coat, purse, and one shoe were missing.

Initial media reports contained lurid details but nothing

that pointed to a suspect. In court records of the trial, however, a full eight years after the killing, there was damning, if circumstantial, evidence implicating officer Kirby. Sheriff Russell testified that he and Kirby had both gone to the scene, observed the girl, and while he went back to his car to call for backup, Kirby walked over shoe prints that were beside the body, effectively destroying them as evidence. He also accused Kirby of having scuffed up tire tracks discovered on a road nearby, prints from the car apparently used to transport the dead girl. Sarah's father had always found those accusations implausible. How could someone with Kirby's obvious intelligence do anything that stupid? Panic? Possibly. But that would have been so far out of character it would strain, if not break, credulity.

Yet the jury, acting on the instructions of the judge and persuaded by the prosecutor's closing arguments, had added up the circumstantial evidence and found Kirby guilty of murder in the second degree. The clincher, apparently, was testimony from a surprise witness who'd come forward after eight years of silence and claimed to have seen the girl get into Kirby's car the night she was murdered.

Other circumstances had troubled Sarah's father. Russell moonlighted as a security guard on important occasions at Caulfield's estate. Kirby was a city cop, a motorcycle officer. During his first year on the force he had presented Kenneth Caulfield with a very public speeding ticket, the only one ever handed him, and the source of embarrassment for the great man, who always got even. Ursula Ketterman's mother had been the Caulfield's laundry woman for more than a decade. She also did laundry for the family of the principal of Keaton School, and worked at his home on Fridays. Ursula had gone missing on a Friday. Timothy Caulfield had attended Keaton for four years, culminating in a two month session of summer school, which ended that same day.

And then Timmy had dropped out of sight.

"Too many unanswered questions, Ernie. Dad could never get this case out of his mind. And he believed, even if he didn't have evidence, that Timmy had somehow been involved.

"And here's another thing; *Time* and LIFE, when they wrote about Kirby being sent to San Quentin, said he'd been arrested on a morals charge after a mother claimed he'd molested her 10 year old son. And as soon as he was behind bars, boom, this Dorothy Carter shows up. Said she hadn't come forward for eight years because she was afraid for her life. Now that Kirby was in jail she felt it was safe. Very convenient. She testified she'd seen Ursula getting into Kirby's car that night.

"Could the Sheriff have set the whole thing up? There are no court records about a morals arrest. The only record Kirby ever had was for a speeding ticket."

The trial continued through the summer of 1951. Kirby

was found guilty and sent to San Quentin state prison.

His motion for a retrial was denied. Kirby adamantly maintained his innocence, but his protestations swam against a rip tide of hostile public opinion. When his wife and children found occasion to speak out in his support, articles in the *Patriot* gave the impression that this was just a loyal and subservient family doing their best to be faithful to an obviously guilty man.

John Westland, Kirby's attorney, appealed the case to the California Supreme Court, stating in his pleading that there was a miscarriage of justice because the verdict was reached due to misconduct by the Deputy District Attorney, and instructions to the jury and rulings of the court that were "prejudicially erroneous."

On October 17, 1952, the California Supreme Court issued a lengthy ruling on the case, citing "flagrant misconduct" and describing remarks of the deputy D.A. as "most reprehensible."

The ruling concluded that there had indeed been a miscarriage of justice in the case, the guilty verdict against Kirby was reversed, and his request for a new trial was granted. Jury selection began almost immediately.

The retrial took less than a week. On January 15, 1953, a new jury, after deliberating the facts of the case for just 14 minutes, reached a "not guilty" verdict. Leonard Kirby walked out of the courthouse a free man. Neither *Time* nor LIFE carried a word about a second trial or

Kirby's acquittal. Nor had there been more than a short paragraph in the police blotter section of the *Patriot*.

"Public guilt and private innocence," Ernie fumed, reading the records. "Professor Jewison would have made a benchmark example of media ethics with this one. And we don't have any idea of who was in bed with whom. All we really know is that Caulfield ran the county back then, and his machinery certainly included the forces of truth and justice."

Louis Els' article in *The Echo* had mentioned the Caulfield's housekeeper. She was not hard to find. Mieke Van der Vick, a gregarious immigrant from Holland, had worked for a total of just five families since she and her husband arrived in California in 1934. A fountain of ebullience, she laughingly dubbed herself "Bad Maid." She worked for the Caulfields for twelve years, and left their employ when Caulfield's eldest daughter moved from Delaware to Tigh Harbor after her youngest, at age eight, contracted polio.

Kenneth Caulfield had insisted that the family take advantage of Tigh Harbor's climate and the amenities of the estate for the child's recuperation. The husband was a naval architect who specialized in Americas Cup racing sloop design. The "Bad Maid" described him as "frustrated by the racing time-out caused by Adolf and Tojo and their damned World War." Apparently, if he could work near one ocean or the other, he felt sane. His wife was a take charge woman, who let the Bad Maid go after a tense sixty days. She gave her an excellent reference, but said to her privately, "there can only be one boss in the house."

Her self confidence undiminished, Mieke now worked for an 80-year old retired banker, who evidently valued her cheery company as much as her cooking and cleaning. In the banker's glassed-in sun room, Meike gave Sarah iced tea, Dutch cookies, and a pot full of information. Sarah learned that shortly before Russell began moonlighting as Caulfield's security guard, he had brought Timothy to the front door late one Saturday night. The boy had been drinking beer with three others and run his Studebaker into an irrigation ditch near the Matsumoto strawberry farm north of town. Deputy Russell, on patrol, came across the scene, found no one injured, and sent the other boys home on foot. He then brought Timothy to his father.

"You'd probably like to keep this sort of quiet, I assume, sir," Russell said.

Caulfield assured him that he was most grateful, and that's all Mieke said she knew about it. "And I knew it happened just like that because Mr. Timothy puked all over the front hall, and I was cleaning up the mess when all this talk was going on."

Another Caulfield skeleton? Sarah mused. "But y'-know, I liked Timmy," Meike continued. "Oh, he was spoiled, sure, but he was a sweet kid, really. He was only eight years old when I came to the family. He liked it when people paid attention to him without always having more important things to do. When he was still little he'd play all day down on the sand with the Ketterman girl, bless her little heart. He'd sit in the kitchen and talk with me sometimes when I was cooking. When he was becoming a teenager it was kind of hard for him, bein' so sensitive and all that, y'know, but it seemed like he got okay about it, y'know, with his hormone things and all that. Boys, y'know.

"Best thing that ever happened was he got to be a real good sailor. I think that was the most important thing ever come out of his schoolin', cause he sure didn't like to study books. But that last summer, goin' off to the other school, now that was different. Strange, even. He'd been the whole summer locked up at Keaton, and y'-know, I think that was real cruel for somebody like Timmy, who just loved bein' hours out on the water. That poor dear Ketterman child loved to sail about as much as him, she did. On laundry days the year before she died she'd come into the kitchen, ask me for some cookies, and then they'd both prance off for the beach and the boat.

"'I'm Timmy's First Mate now,' she'd boast, with the biggest ever grin. She was so happy. What a terrible, terrible, thing that was. Just unbelievable, really. Then Timmy come back home after those summer classes and he never touched his boat again, never even went down to the boathouse. He went away to that other school, and that was the strangest thing of all. He was back home in just a few days; and really, y'know, I think he must'a caught some kind of fever up there that made him real tense, real nervous. I guess he'd kinda gone out of his head. They'd had to bring him back home. The doctor come over several times, y'know, and gave him medicine to calm him down. I took him a meal just once early on, but then it was always his mother that done it. It was weird what he said when I give him the tray that time."

"What did he say, Meike?" Sarah asked, as casually as she could.

"Well, he looked at me real strange, and scared-like, and then he said, 'I didn't tell Garth. I didn't!' He kept sayin' it over and over until I left the room. I told his mother about it, and after that she took him his meals.

"Pretty soon he got taken in the plane to have his nerves treated, I think. He come back home for a bit before he went away to recuperate. His folks would talk about him. I couldn't understand all they were sayin', though, to be honest, I always tried to hear things; the Bad Maid is just there, you know, like a chair in the corner. It's what makes life interesting, isn't it?"

She sat back and laughed. Then suddenly stopped; "But they talked about Timmy like he was just a chair in a corner, too, like he wasn't really there anymore. Russell helped out in those days, and took him up to the ranch,"

For another half hour the gregarious Mrs. van der Vyck

160

filled in the tapestry of life at the Caulfields in full color. It was a household of dinner parties, formal and informal receptions, important people, fine food, politics.

"Who came to all those events?" Sarah asked.

"Oh, lots of people," Mieke enthused. "O'course, some were regulars. The district attorney, judges, the sheriff. They were almost always there. And people from Sacramento, congressmen, lots of others. There was always a security guard when there was an event, Deputy Russell, he was Mr. Caulfield's man for that, but o'course when he got to be Sheriff, he was at the parties with everybody else."

"Who was Garth," Ernie wondered aloud that evening. "He was obviously someone Timmy knew, or at least knew of, and he was afraid of him." They were trying to fit the pieces together, sitting on the bent oak chairs in *The Echo's* "war room," which apart from Sarah's glassed off cubicle, was its only room. A lot of pieces were missing, but a few looked like they might connect to the puzzle. Had Garth been a student? Unlikely. The Keaton yearbooks for 1939 through 1942 yielded no clue.

"Maybe he just wasn't a Keaton School type," Sarah opined.

The records of Tigh Harbor High School for the class of 1940 showed 368 girls and 331 boys.

"My little sister graduated that year," the school secretary exclaimed to Ernie across the counter of the school's office. "I remember we sat on the aisle for the procession at the ceremony, and our little brother threw a grasshopper at her. Mama hit him on the ear and he started crying. But nobody heard him, because the record was loud and a lot of parents were crying anyway. She was a rebel, my sister, and we didn't know if she'd ever make it through to graduation. We were really proud, I can tell you."

"That's great," Ernie said, "Where is she now?"

"Well, you may not believe this, Mr. Hemmingway, but my little sister lives in Manley Ranch, she has four kids, she's still married to her first husband, who's a doctor of tropical diseases, and she's on the Board of Education! How's that for a success story? Yes, maybe that's a story for your paper."

"It might well be," Ernie answered. "If I don't find who I'm looking for in the records you've got here, I'll look her up."

Ernie didn't find him. Maybe he was there and just didn't show, he mused. First names can be a pain. Maybe Garth was a nickname, short for Gerard or Geronimo or some other name the guy couldn't live with.

Sure enough, the school clerk's sister did remember him, very well, in fact.

"Oh man," she said, holding her toddler on her hip while she deftly fed supper to the other three at the kitchen counter of her stuccoed Manley Ranch tract home. She put the two-year-old in a high chair.

"Marty, you look after Arthur for a few minutes while I talk with this gentleman on the patio. There's a nice dessert tonight, kidlets, and Daddy will be here before storytime."

On the patio she motioned Ernie to a chair and sat down herself, arching her back as if she'd just run a long race.

"Oh man, Mr. Hemmingway. you're from Oak Hills? Has something serious happened? Is he in trouble again? Oh man, just the name of Garth Rothaker gives me chills."

"Why's that, Mrs. Nanton?"

"Well, just between you and me and everybody else in Tigh Harbor, Garth Rothaker was wild as a bull, and I was fascinated by him. There were two other guys and three of us girls and we were our own brand of Hells Angels. The guys had Harley's and on weekends we'd cruise the coast. Sometimes we didn't get back until late Monday, and my folks just had a cow. They had enough cows over me to start a dairy farm."

"Do you know where he is now?" Ernie asked.

"Not a clue. In fact, the Angels blew up in my face at Christmas that year. Garth got smashed out of his mind, brawled with some guy in the alley out alongside the "Y," and almost killed the jerk. They locked him up for thirty days."

"What was the fight all about?"

"Well, I think the guy called him Garfield. He hated the name, even if that's what he was christened. It was his dad's name, too, and oh, how he hated that man. But Garth never came back to school. Lotta people said the roof was gonna blow off at graduation when the year-book came out. It would list him as Garfield in broad daylight. Somebody told me he'd joined the Marines just to avoid it. Anyway, by graduation, he was nowhere around, and for me, that's the best thing that could have happened."

The Veteran's administration in West Los Angeles was surprisingly open about giving information. Ernie learned that Garfield Rothaker had enlisted in the United States Navy on February 14, 1942. It was a Valentine Ernie was glad to receive. Garth opted for Marine training, which he received at Camp Pendleton in San Diego County. He had been the boxing champion of the base, and evidently seen the inside of the brig on more than one occasion. In September of '42 he had shipped out to the Pacific the-ater, served in several island campaigns with the 5th divi-sion, and was wounded in the shoulder by a mortar fragment during the landing on Iwo Jima. He received an honorable discharge on June 4, 1945 at the Presidio in San Francisco. Address given was the Armed Forces Service Center in Portland, Oregon.

By now completely ignoring the phone company charges for long distance, Ernie called the Center, which had been mothballed for nearly five years, then reactivated as a resource for veterans during the Korean War. The files for 1945, the volunteer told Ernie on the phone, were dusty but available. Garth had worked as a longshoreman in the Portland harbor until 1951, when he moved to the nearby town of Vernonia. There was no forwarding address.

"I'll have to go there," Ernie told Sarah that evening. "We may be looking for a needle in a haystack, but at least we've found the haystack. There's a flight to Portland at noon tomorrow from San Francisco. I'll leave my car there and get a rental in Oregon. And I've been saving, Sarah, so don't worry about costs; I haven't had many expenses since I came to *The Echo*."

"That's very generous, Ernie. I'll go up to Little Sequoia and see what I can learn. It's only a mile from Caulfield's ranch, and somebody there is sure to have seen Timmy. We're really getting somewhere!" Then she saw he was frowning.

"What? you don't think I can handle a place like Little Sequoia? It's not Chicago, you know."

"I know, but it's a hair-raising three-hour drive up the Rattlesnake highway; besides, you don't know who talks to whom in a place like that."

"Oh, c'mon, Ernie, it's just a wide spot in the road. But you're sweet to be concerned about me, and I promise you, I'll be careful."

Ernie called United and booked his flight.

* * * *

Sarah liked to drive. Getting behind the wheel had always been a pleasure, ever since her father had put her on his lap when she was 12 and let her steer down the lane from the house on occasion. She'd had her own car since she was in college, had driven rentals in cities all over the western states, and heck, she thought, I've even cruised around Paris.

Ernie was still pensive next morning as he watched Sarah drive away from *The Echo*. One thing she doesn't lack, he mused, is confidence. But I've got a plane to catch.

Sarah shifted frequently as the car snaked up the torturous highway, with its sharp turns and sheer drop-offs. The river 600 feet below ran all year, in summer a trout stream fed by mountain springs, in winter a torrent fed by runoff from Pacific storms. The road was aptly named, and not a few travelers had felt its venom. But it was the only route from the coast over the Santa Lucia Range to the highlands.

The small welcome sign for Little Sequoia showed through Sarah's windshield just two hours and thirty eight minutes from the time she left Oak Hills, she noted with a smile. A Flying "A" service station with a single pump stood sentinel at the crossroads. Just beside it was a store. A sign by the door advertised Copenhagen Chewing Tobacco, Scott Toilet Paper, and Burpee's Seeds, guaranteed to grow. A neon sign in the window declared that Pabst Blue Ribbon Beer was available, along with the grocery basics on the shelves. This place was 14 miles away from anywhere, which would be "Greater" Sequoia, farther east.

Ten gallons of gas for starters, Sarah decided. She wondered if they had anything to clean the windshield with. If not, the bugs that sacrificed themselves on the way up the Rattlesnake would just have to stay stuck. She looked inside the station and saw no one. Then she heard a screen door slam. "I'll pump your gas," came a voice behind her. The woman might have been about Sarah's age, but looked older. She grabbed the pump handle, rocked it back and forth, and the red colored fuel poured into the glass tube until the gauge read ten. Then she drained it into the car, lifting the hose from the pump down to the nozzle to get it all out. Capable, Sarah thought. But windshields were not part of the service. They went into the store and Sarah picked up an Almond Joy and a Dr. Pepper. She paid the girl, who said she'd lived around here all her life, well, in Sequoia really.

"I drive out here at six in the morning every day 'cept Sunday. There's a spurt of business from six to seven, then things quiet down. Late in the afternoon, that's when mostly guys from the ranches come in for beer 'n stuff, hang around 'til they have to get back for dinner, or maybe just stay. That's the best part of this job. During most of the day I take care of orderin' and stockin' stuff for Jennings. He owns the station, but he'd rather tinker with his Jeep and his Harley than wait on human bein's, the old fart. He's okay, though. Hires me to run things.

"Me? Doin' this for twelve years, since I was eighteen. I keep the place open during the day for the odd customer, like I don't mean like you're odd or nuthin'. But most people around here are out in the field all day. Timothy Caulfield? Couldn't say. The Caulfield place is about four miles back down the road, up on the ridge, say it's the biggest spread in the county. Even got a landing strip up there next to the Russell Ranch. Why you askin'?"

With the equivalent of an electric shock, Sarah suddenly realized she had not prepared a "why" to explain her presence in Little Sequoia.

"Well, my brother went to school with Timmy and then moved up north and lost touch. Wondered if he might live somewhere around here now."

"Beats me. Never had no Caulfields come by, least when I been here."

"Well, it was a long shot anyway. I'll tell my bro he'll have to try somewhere else to find his friend. What's your name? Annie? I like that, I had an Aunt Annie once, my dad told me, but I never met her. Better head back down the hill. It's getting late. That Rattlesnake's quite a road, isn't it?"

Sarah started her engine, furious with herself for not having prepared a cover story for driving up and then right back down the Rattlesnake. She hoped she hadn't raised a red flag.

Annie leaned against the door and watched Sarah drive away, then picked up the phone and dialed a number.

"Bunk house."

"Lemme talk to Bull."

Briefly Annie described Sarah's visit and questions. "Fuck!" she heard. "You say she came up the hill and went back down? What kinda car she drivin'? What color? Shit." The phone went dead.

Bull Haymore ran out of the bunkhouse and climbed into a dark blue 1955 Chevrolet pickup. It had deep tread tires, stiff shocks, and a modified suspension that made it ride high for field work. A heavy steel push type grille was welded onto the front of the chassis. Two high intensity headlamps were fitted above the grille. Haymore fired up the powerful V8 and threw dirt behind him for forty feet as he raced out of the bunkhouse yard. He reached the top of the ridge just as the sun was setting, but there was still enough light down the mountain to show where the Rattlesnake began its twisting path into the canyon. He saw the tail lights of a car disappear around the curve.

Rattlesnake Canyon is so narrow that the weather is different at the bottom, like the grand Canyon in Arizona, but not as severe. In some places, the river is a thousand feet below the ridge at the top. The roadway, for the most part, runs about 500 feet above the river, principally because the engineers found that the most efficient path when they started blasting the route at the turn of the century. Before that, settlers, ranchers and travelers navigated the canyon on a clay and gravel road directly beside the river. Nobody traveled the canyon at flood stage. You either had your beans and bacon stocked up for the season or went without.

Sarah had driven about ten miles into the canyon, her mind moving a great deal faster than her car. By now she'd muzzled her concern about her lack of a "story." And hey, Ernie, that didn't turn out to be a dry hole, did it? I think we struck oil! I had no idea Russell has a place up here. There's even an airstrip! I just thought Russell might have been in and out of Caulfield's spread. That Annie was sure a kick. Sounds like she gives the boys a good time after work. Well, it's dead up there during the day. Imagine working 12 years in a place like that.

It was almost dark in the gorge; only a trickle of light spilled down from the dusk above. Suddenly, immediately behind her, light blazed like the sun. The brilliance blinded her. A vehicle was so tight on her bumper it seemed to engulf her. Then it rammed into the back of her car, just as she was heading into a curve.

My God, he's trying to kill me!

Almost automatically Sarah shifted down and floored

the accelerator. She shot ahead but was quickly caught, and she heard the roar of a powerful engine. The truck smashed into her again, and again. Now she was perilously close to losing control on the hairpin turns. The drop off was bottomless here, and only a four foot shoulder separated her from the brink. Her attacker's obvious intent was to drive her over the edge. He was pushing her closer and closer to the drop off. An image of flying through the air flashed into her mind when suddenly there were tail lights in front of her. A station wagon was stopped, partly on the road, partly on the narrow shoulder. There were people beside it, kneeling by the right rear tire. Instantly she swerved in front of the wagon and screeched to a stop. The death machine behind her had no choice but to overtake her. Brakelights blazed and smoke billowed from all four tires as it slid to a halt. Her headlights showed the driver, looking back, and she gasped in horror at a face eerily like the one that terrified her that day she ran for her life through the cemetery. Slowly the driver turned his head and moved on.

Sarah started to shake. Her heart was racing. A face appeared at her window and she screamed in terror. Then she realized it was someone from the station wagon. Still quivering, she opened the window.

"Are you all right, ma'am? asked the man. "What was that all about?"

"I—" She couldn't talk. Her throat, the muscles of her neck, all seemed in spasm.

"Just a minute, ma'am. I'll get my wife."

She was a kind, capable lady, who worked in a fabric store in San Luis Obispo and wore a cheerful yellow hat. She and her husband and eight year old son had been in Sequoia for a week visiting her ailing parents. They had taken their son out of third grade for the week because it may be the last recollection he would have of his granny.

"Life and death don't always announce themselves, honey," the lady said after Sarah had calmed her racing heart. "Sometimes they don't give you any warning at all. Of course we've been talking about Freddie and his Grandma. But who'd have thought a flat tire could mean life for someone you'd never met?"

Sarah, finished with the shaking now and nourished by the orange young Freddie had peeled for her, hugged the lady with the yellow hat, hugged her husband, and hugged her son. In their wagon they followed her down the mountain, and at Oak Hills stayed with her until she was safely home. None of them noticed the pickup parked on a side road near the city limits with its lights off, the driver watching.

* * * *

Finding out about Garth Rothaker was less of a problem than Ernie anticipated. Everyone in Vernonia knew stories about that wild man, it seemed. But the mechanic at the town's sole gas station/garage had definitive information. Garth had been in and out of jail, and involved in lots of brawls, he told Ernie. He had died a year ago when he was fall-down drunk and tried to climb the 40-degree hillside behind the fire station on his raked Harley. The beast got away from him, rolled three times on the way down, and landed on the gravel parking lot with the gear shift foot lever going right through his skull. The whole three-man fire department saw the exhibition—and the execution. Garth's brother came from California and took the body.

Brother? Ernie was driving south on a twisty road now toward Timber and Buxton. Vernonia had once been the site of a bustling lumber mill, but the disastrous Tillamook Burn of the early thirties had nearly turned it into a ghost town. Legend said enough timber burned then to rebuild every house from Portland to San Francisco. Even ghosts could have trouble with these twists, Ernie mused. But the banked curves might have been an engineering achievement in the 1920s. At least there aren't canyons or drop-offs here like the Rattlesnake. He wondered how it had gone for Sarah in Little Sequoia. He'd worried about her going up there on her own. But she's a big girl, as she keeps telling me.

At Buxton, he headed east on a straighter road to the mighty Columbia, and back north along the river to St. Helens, the county seat of Columbia County. Garth Rothaker had not been brought there after he died, but the records were at the County Court House, an unremarkable square structure of red cut stone that hadn't seen a great deal of improvement since it was built in the twenties. The coroner's office gave him the address of a Benjamin Rothaker of San Jose, California, who had taken receipt of the body of Garth Rothaker in Vernonia on June 27 of the prior year. Benjamin had driven from San Jose towing a trailer built from the bed of an old Ford pickup. He had navigated the corkscrew road to Vernonia without incident, and evidently returned to California with the wooden casket of his brother on board.

Outside the courthouse Ernie reflected: he had come to the Northwest to follow a lead and found a dead man and perhaps a dead end. But maybe the brother in San Jose could tell him more. He could smell the pines and firs that seemed to grow like wildflowers in the desert after rain. But of course it rained here most of the time, Sarah had lamented. Everything grew here. To the northeast he could see Mt. St. Helens, one of the dormant volcanoes that formed a majestic necklace along the Pacific coast. Those were violent days of nature, he thought; these were violent days of human nature.

* * * *

Benji Rothaker lived alone in a small, well-tended house in San Jose, in a row of small well-tended houses. He worked for a regional phone company and was researching new technologies. He spoke openly and frankly, almost Ernie thought, as if he'd been expecting this visit. Three years younger than Garth, Benji was intelligent, soft spoken and had a pleasant smile. He was only a year behind Garth in school. From as long back as he could remember, he had worshiped his fearless brother, admired his arrogance and antics in their school years, but in his junior year of high school had made an about face.

There was no evangelist crusading in Tigh Harbor at the time. There was only the conversation with his brother on the first day of September, sitting in the empty bleachers of the football field at Tigh Harbor High School. Garth was home on a 10-day pass prior to shipping out to the Pacific theater. They were smoking pot, drinking beers that Garth had "liberated" from Bales Cash Store by putting them in the grocery store's trash, then collecting them out back after closing time.

Up until that moment, Benjamin, reticent by nature, had imagined himself duplicating his brother's bravado, getting the women, reveling in the vicarious thrill of always living just over the edge. His parents were extravagantly proud of Benjamin, and just as extravagantly dismayed with his brother. They had given up on Garth five years before, after the night they told him he had to be home by 10 p.m. Enraged by the curfew, Garth had slashed the kitchen cupboards with a butcher knife. He was then in the ninth grade. From that time on, Garth was in control of his family, and to the best of his ability to intimidate, in control of everyone he touched.

That night on the bleachers, Garth had boasted to Benjamin about "having" Ursula Ketterman. It was two days after her body had been found. She'd made too much noise, he'd said, and the bitch's gotta learn to shut it up. Then he relived for his hero-worshipping 16-year old brother every detail of the killing.

"Bull and me fucked her good," he'd announced. Bragging about it made him feel like a real big shot, Benjamin said.

Deeply tormented by what he had learned on the bleachers, Benjamin had left their home sometime after midnight and made his way to the bay. At the beach just a few feet from the old wooden pier that housed the lobster restaurant, he had walked into the water until he was up to his neck, then gone under and stayed under for as long as he could hold his breath. He emerged from the ocean, ". . . changed, I guess. I knew I was at a crossroads, that if I didn't go a different way, I'd die as a human being, even if I kept on living as a human animal."

The next night was September 2. Benji said Garth had somehow dragged himself home about midnight, badly beaten. He had broken ribs, deep cuts, bruises from blows to his head, and was minus his front teeth. He would say nothing about what happened. The next day he had hitchhiked back to camp.

Lordy, Ernie mused, who could have mauled Garth like that, the Garth who was afraid of no one? Whoever it was certainly knew the truth about the murder of Ursula Ketterman, truth never revealed until now. And why never revealed? Why, Benji?

"He was my brother."

Ernie took notes on everything Benji told him about the murder. Garth had griped that those "snot-nosed Keaton kids" had been getting it for weeks, every Friday, when the girl's mother came to do laundry for the school principal. Garth learned of the ritual on Wednesday, his third day home on leave. He was at Blye Billiards in the early evening, shooting pool and looking for some action from the gaggle of locals present. A few regulars were swapping stories at the bar. Billy Temple and a half dozen would-be pool sharks, including Georgie Baker, home on leave from Navy Boot Camp, were playing nine-ball at a table in the back. Several about to graduate high school seniors, Randy Russo among them, were partying ahead of receiving their diplomas. Well oiled by too many underage beers, Randy was putting on a show, letting loose because he had only two more days of school and then he'd be out of that "damned hell hole."

"But God, I'll miss the Friday fucks," he'd said. It didn't take long for Garth, the inquisitor, to find out what he meant.

* * * *

Ernie recognized he had a problem. And it wasn't a little one. Back when he had discovered Martin's two-timing, Ernie had locked away the knowledge for weeks. It was his nature not to say a great deal. He could write more easily than he could verbalize, at least about his emotions. He would take a fact, massage it, pass it through a

177

number of cerebral considerations, and bring it out at the time and place it seemed appropriate, useful, not hurtful, etc. He knew this was an aspect of his personality, and also that it was a convenient place to hide. He had waited to tell Sarah about the photo of Martin with the call girl at the Bonaventure in Los Angeles, but that had been the right thing to do, he reasoned, because he was not about to be the one who would drive a wedge between her and her husband, even if he wished the guy would get hit by a train.

In truth, it wasn't that he didn't want to be the one to pry them apart. It was just that he didn't want her ever to think he had told her so he could have her for himself. God, Ernie, why didn't you keep awake during those psychology lectures? Now here he was again. Benji seemed to have held back nothing of what he knew about the murder of Ursula Ketterman.

Benji had no idea that one single element of the story he related, beyond even the savage taking of a young girl's life, had hit Ernie like a physical blow. He was still massaging it when he wearily walked into *The Echo* office at noon the next day and heard Sarah's report of the Rattlesnake chase.

"Oh my God!" Ernie exclaimed, "you could have been in the bottom of that canyon and not found for days! Thank heaven you're okay." He hugged her, took her in his arms, pressed her cheek to his face, ran his hand through her hair. He didn't say I told you so, but boiling under his gratitude he thought it, angry with himself that he had let her go despite his misgivings. Then, when he described for Sarah his meeting with Benjamin, he did it carefully, without referring to his notes. It took him half an hour to tell her the parts of the story he chose for her to hear.

"Garth had hitchhiked home on leave. He was hanging out with a ranch hand named Bull who owned a beat up truck and was a hellraiser like himself. The prospect of having Ursula on a platter really set them off. We don't know exactly what Randy said about the Friday afternoons in the greenhouse, but it was obviously enough to get them there. Randy wasn't even at school that day. The test papers had already been graded, and he couldn't get out of there fast enough. But he must have told Garth that Timmy was going to be at the school one last time that Friday with Ursula.

"When Garth and Bull walked into the greenhouse, Timmy was there with another guy, talking with Ursula by the tool racks, and they were all looking serious. The guy and Timmy were telling Ursula that they all had to get out of there *right now!* Garth said they were just heading for the door when he walked over to her, put his hands on her breasts and saw her mouth drop open in shock. 'You shoulda seen her,' he'd bragged with a sneer. She screamed at him to stop it, but he didn't, and she started clawing at him, scratched at his face with her fingernails and kept on screaming. Timmy and the other guy lunged at him and yelled, and then Bull barged in and cried, "Fuck off, Pansies." Bull slugged the guy on the side of the head and knocked him into Timmy. They landed in a heap on the gravel. The guy staggered up and tried to come back at Garth, but Bull grabbed him, hit him in the gut this time and threw him back on Timmy, and when he got up Bull came at him again and knocked him cold. Timmy just took off. Ursula fought like a tiger, but when they had finished with her and still couldn't keep her quiet, they strangled her."

"Animals! Animals! My God, Ernie, they aren't human beings. they're animals!"

"Worse, Sarah. Animals wouldn't do that." She turned to look out the window, searching for light and air. "Those two little cowards knew all along who killed her and they never said anything!"

"Yes, and even if those two weren't there to hurt her, they couldn't stop it from happening." He was quiet a minute, shivered slightly, and then said, "I guess that's the end of it."

"What? Ernie! What do you mean, the end of it? Who was that other guy? And where has Timmy been for the last 13 years? We've got to find the truth, Ernie. The whole truth."

"That's what I love about you Sarah. You throw your life at everything you do. Of course at some point, you'll have to let this go."

"What do you mean by that?"

"Well, just that."

"Ernie, you know we haven't got the whole truth yet. Isn't that what we're after? Isn't that the way to bury Caulfield?"

"Yes, but Caulfield's been buried for years and we're still looking for coffin nails."

He realized it was not an impressive argument.

* * * *

The Rattlesnake chase made it clear that Russell was important to the story. Sarah called her brother in San Jose to quiz him on what an officer who'd been involved in a case that was many years old might be thinking. She didn't tell him that she'd been looking for clues about what had happened to his childhood friend Timmy Caulfield. Later she thought a lot about that.

"We're working on a big story, Georgie, something that happened a long time ago, and we think in some way it involves a guy who used to be a cop. What do cops think about when they're retired, and don't you dare tell me it's women."

When Sarah didn't hear an immediate chuckle at this from her brother, she wondered for a moment if the phone was working. Then, "Well it's nothing out of the ordinary, Sarah. I'd think most of the time about my own kids, and hope to God they wouldn't end up like some of the trash we have to deal with. If the guy's older, he's probably thinking about his grandkids."

* * * *

Kenneth Caulfield had owned an airplane since 1938, and was the first publisher on the coast after William Randolph Hearst to boast such a luxury. Harry Chandler, owner of the Los Angeles Times, didn't even have a private plane. But Caulfield lived far from an airline hub. A sidebar in the memorial edition of the *Patriot* told how he considered his twin-tailed Beechcraft the third best business tool he ever had at his disposal, after his typewriter and telephone.

Caulfield was often in Sacramento, San Francisco, and Los Angeles. He had a VFR pilot's license, and while he enjoyed flying almost as much as riding his champion Argentine-bred horses, he employed a full-time captain. After a dozen phone calls, Ernie tracked down Walley Elliston, Caulfield's pilot from the early forties, now a senior captain with Pan American Airways, flying Lockheed Super "G" Constellations on the San Francisco-Tokyo-Singapore route every three weeks. Elliston, a carefully groomed Erroll Flynn look alike, lived in Marin County, in a comfortable home with an arched picture window that overlooked San Francisco Bay. He was obviously enjoying himself.

"I've always loved life," Elliston declared, "always loved flying."

Borrowing again from *Sunset's* Kathy Stroud, Ernie told Elliston he was writing a history of leading West Coast families and had driven north to see him because of Kenneth Caulfield. The possible notoriety was not lost on Elliston, who promptly offered Ernie a drink, his time, and a chair on the patio.

"I'd bet you have some interesting stories to tell about important people who've been on your plane and places you've flown to, Captain. Where did you take Mr. Caulfield most of the time?"

"Well, we usually stayed in California. L.A., 'Frisco, and of course plenty of trips to Sacramento; Mr. Caulfield was really involved in politics and I guess he did a lot of arm twisting in the capitol. I know he had other businesses as well as newspapers. He was always telling me about something he'd be bringing home for Tigh Harbor from Sacramento or Washington. He was even a U.S. Senator, did you know that?"

"I do believe I heard, Captain. You certainly moved around in - uh - high places. Did you fly him back to Washington sometimes?"

"Only once. As luck would have it, we hit rough weather over Kansas, and after that he flew commercial whenever he went East. That Beechcraft was a good little plane for its time, but a far cry from a Super Connie. I was back there one other time while I worked for him, and it was smooth as silk. He should have been on that flight."

"What flight was that?"

"Ha! that's a trip I won't forget. It turned into a holiday! It was when Mr. Caulfield's son was so sick."

"Oh?"

"Yeah, he had to go for some kind of treatment in Connecticut. It was October 9, on my birthday. I remember old Doc Milosovic brought him to the airport in an ambulance. We'd had the plane fitted to hold the gurney tight during the flight, emergency equipment in case he needed it. But he just seemed to be asleep, like he'd had a knockout pill. Guess he needed the treatment all right. We'd flown to San Francisco to get him a couple weeks before."

"Really? What was he doing in San Francisco?"

"Oh, he was up at a Junior College. Yeah, I took Mr. Caulfield and the doctor up there to bring him home. They didn't talk to me about what was the matter with him, but from what I overheard I think it was something mental. I gathered he'd gone off his rocker up there, climbed a flagpole or something. Maybe he was scared of getting drafted, I dunno. Whatever he was imagining, the kid was really sick. We flew him east for treatment. There was a paramedic went along with him. Said he was a cop as well. Anyway it was a smooth flight all the way to Stamford, which was the closest airport to Greenwich, where the clinic was. Must have been a smooth ride to the hospital too— never saw a Cadillac ambulance or one with roses painted on it before.

But the reason I remember that trip so well was that instead of flying right back, Mr. Caulfield had me wait until his son was well enough to come home. You imagine that? Went up to Maine, ate lobster, sailed at Martha's Vineyard, saw shows in New York—I saw the thousandth performance of *Babes In Arms!* Never forget it. Must have been three weeks, all expenses included, until the boy was ready. The flight back was bizarre though. The kid still had bandages on his head. Guess he was better, but he was strange, just sat there and stared. It was weird, because he had always been real polite and courteous. Maybe they did brain surgery on him. Of course he had some recuperating to do, but at least he wasn't on a stretcher anymore. Probably didn't take long for him to get back to his old self. We took him up to the mesa."

"Where was that?" Ernie asked, casually.

"It was a place he could recuperate. Tiny little landing strip on the edge of the Caulfield spread. Not even on the map. I remember I had to side-slip in to land. Take off was easy though, without the weight. Mr. Caulfield got himself a Cessna after I told him I'd be leaving to ferry B-17s over to Europe. That little high-wing flivver of his could easy get in and out of that cowpatch at the ranch. He said he wanted to take his boy up in the plane, show him the countryside."

Ernie called Sarah from a coffee shop just north of the Golden Gate Bridge and passed on all he'd learned. He

185

wanted to drive straight through to Oak Hills, but soon realized that wasn't a good idea. From a motel south of San Francisco he called Sarah again. "This is one pooped reporter," he announced. They reviewed the day's discoveries; Sarah had learned from the county assessor that Caulfield sold Sheriff Russell 200 acres on the southeast corner of his property just six weeks after the murder. "How's that for coincidence?"

"The landing strip, the address of the undertaker, the pieces fit together," Ernie said.

"And now we've got the name of a doctor," Sarah enthused before signing off. "With a name like 'Old Doc Milosovic,' he shouldn't be hard to track down."

Sarah immediately phoned Carrie Edmonds, the loquacious 62-year-old society columnist of the former Tigh Harbor *Sentinel,* and learned the Milosovic name held a lingering celebrity. Edmonds was more than ready, eager even, to "tell all" to George Baker's daughter.

"Come tomorrow."

Next morning Sarah drove down the hill to meet with Edmonds. She took copious notes.

* * * *

Doc Milosovic had one son, Vernon. Doc was in his fifties when the boy was born. Vernon was coddled by a powerful, possessive mother and largely ignored by a father who drank too much. In his mid-20s, Vernon had

186

been manager of the local YMCA, until late in the summer of 1939 when he scandalized Tigh Harbor by getting arrested in Hollywood for propositioning a plainclothes policeman on Sunset Boulevard. The officer was "a beautiful young man," Edmonds told Sarah, and had played bit parts in movies, but couldn't make it as an actor. He did just fine, however, as a cop. Vernon was attending the 1939 Western States Youth Services Convention, held that year at Hollywood's Roosevelt Hotel, and had gone on the prowl after the final banquet.

"Oh the things I know, Sarah, that sadly, your daddy would never let me put in print." Carrie's popular columns gave her access to Tigh Harbor's leading lights. There were dozens of events at the Caulfield estate, some political, most of them social. Her coverage of Caulfield eventually tapered to a minimum, however, not because of editorial direction from George Baker, but because she thought Caulfield's civic and philanthropic activities were largely self-serving.

"Donating a chunk of land, Sarah?" Edmonds exclaimed. "Why does a man give property to a college? Benevolence? No! It's to have his name on some building for the rest of time! We're all mortals and very aware of it. We want to outlive ourselves if we can.

"Interesting about young Timothy, though. You know, don't you, that he was the only son of Angela, Caulfield's second wife? I think Kenneth loved her more than his first wife, and suffered for a long time after she died. She was a very sweet woman, not pretentious at all. Caulfield felt closer to Timmy than to any of his older children, I think, partly because Angela had been so dear. He also was proud of having fathered the boy when he was over 50. But that's no big deal, child, believe me. There are lots of gentlemen around town who could knock you up in their seventies, so beware."

"I'll be careful," Sarah answered, laughing her way out the door.

Sarah knew she'd just had one of the more entertaining interviews of her life. She'd also raked in a pile of valuable information. She headed up the road to Oak Hills. So Daddy knew more about Caulfield than he was willing to print! She knew that, of course; he'd told her he'd never get into a you-started-it-no-you-started-it fight. And these were deep, personal matters.

She pondered "the Ernie Question." She'd made it tougher than it should have been.

I'm supposed to be a take-charge kind of girl. I always get what I want. Even Ernie says so. So why hasn't he ever made love to me? That's not too difficult to answer; he's old school top to bottom, the ask-her-father, wait-till-your-wedding-night school. But Ernie, my love, this is 1956. You need a nudge.

* * * *

The search for the mysterious Garth had led to one murderer, but didn't close the case. Garth was dead, but where was Bull? And what was the real story of Timothy Caulfield? Ursula Ketterman was killed in 1942; Timmy was buried in the cemetery above Tigh Harbor just last year. Where had he been for those fourteen years? Perspective needed.

Refreshed from a good night's sleep in a not so good motel, Ernie drove south on highway 101 and cut to the coast just past the sprawling Hunter Liggett Military reservation. The great metropolis of Sequoia quickly came and went, with Little Sequoia hardly a blink. Then came the Rattlesnake. Ernie shivered involuntarily as he started down the canyon. He drove with caution, and looked in his mirror more than once.

He reviewed the facts: less than a month ago, someone tried to kill Sarah on this highway. But who? The only person she'd talked to was "Annie," the girl at the gas station. Sarah drove away and was attacked twenty minutes later about where I am right now. The deputy in Oak Hills recorded her report of the assault, took pictures of the smashed rear end of her car, but declared that trying to find the truck could take months and might be impossible; everybody up on the highlands drove pickups. Sarah said she'd heard that line before.

Ernie realized now that a single lie told to the police by Ursula Ketterman's mother ten years ago about the circumstances of the girl's disappearance had set the murder case completely off track. The woman must have feared for her job so much that she'd lied to avoid a scandal for a client. Her husband was unable to work then so she'd had to keep earning money. Had she told such a big lie? Big enough to make sure the police overlooked the hours that mattered, the afternoon hours when the murder had taken place.

Caulfield's pilot had seen *Babes in Arms* in New York. The show premiered in 1937, so the thousandth performance would have been in late 1942. That fit. Sarah had tracked down the rose-festooned ambulance, which turned out to be the luxury transporter of the Rose Garden Institute, an upscale treatment center for the mentally ill. Sounds as accessible as Fort Knox. Sarah keeps saying we've got to have bulletproof evidence. Oh, sure. You'd only get that from the Rose Garden Institute by breaking into it!

* * * *

Ernie assured himself, for the umpteenth time, that he did not hate Kenneth Caulfield. But closing the Ketterman murder investigation meant finding out whether or not Caulfield's son had been involved. Ernie could think of only three ways to obtain that kind of evidence: by subpoena from a judge; by witnesses coming forward; by stealing it.

So much for options. We've bet the farm on this "Blaze of Glory" investigation. It's literally all there is. I don't have to drag Sarah to bed to assure our future together.

190

But embark on a life of crime–?

Ernie had been cautious with Sarah since her profane-married-woman proposal. It was so she could never say he took advantage of her when she was on the bounce from Martin. He was used to protecting himself, he knew. But God, he desired her.

Ernie got back to town at five that afternoon and found a formal looking envelope on his desk. It was addressed to E. M. Hemmingway Esq., and in the corner was written, *"By Hand."* nice touch. He opened it and read: *The pleasure of your company is requested for dinner this evening at the home of Miss Sarah Baker. Casual attire. Cocktails at 7.*

I'll be damned, Ernie thought, noting the "Miss."

He showed up on Sarah's porch in tan washable slacks (he did his own laundry) and a cream colored short sleeved shirt (it had been a warm day). He brought his hostess a colorful bouquet from the Cardenas market, which sold flowers year round. It was Friday, and the shop girl gave him a little smile when he made his purchase. Sarah, in a blonde sleeveless dress, welcomed him, expressed delight with the gift, and kissed him lightly on the cheek. She gave him a little smile, too, but hers came with a jolt. He wasn't much of a drinker, but accepted a single malt Bushmills Irish whisky, green label, which Sarah said her father had purchased.

"He didn't drink much either, Ernie, so when he did,

he figured it might as well be the good stuff." They walked out onto the porch, and Ernie was struck at once by the sunset color on the weathered barn to their right and the enormous cottonwood to their left. The yard was shaded by the house, but the property glowed with yellow evening light.

"C'mon," Sarah said, and walked over to the cottonwood. Twenty feet above the ground a large branch stretched out toward the barn, and a wide swing hung from it.

"When we moved here, Daddy put this swing up for me. Elena and I loved it. It had a cowhide seat then that hugged our little butts just right." That smile again. Oh-kay.

"But pretty soon Dad realized it would be nice if mother could use it, too. So he made a special seat for her, real easy to handle. See? It's two feet wide, padded with horsehair and covered with leather. C'mon."

She took Ernie's arm and sat him on the swing, then squeezed next to him and started swinging. "C'mon, Ernie, you've gotta swing too, or it'll be uneven." They both had drinks, and she put her arm through his, and they swung (a little) and drank from linked arms and laughed. Ernie didn't quite know what to think, but knew very well what he was feeling.

Dinner was fresh halibut, hauled in early that morning to Morro Bay by the local fishing fleet, then included in the daily delivery to the Cardenas store in Oak Hills. There was fresh asparagus and small red potatoes from Papa Beto's fields, a nicely layered '52 Sauvignon Blanc from Napa Valley, blackberry crisp with ice cream, and Irish coffee followed by an excellent port from Spain.

"Good lord, Sarah, I'm overcome. And without a doubt, overstuffed. I don't know when I've had such a wonderful dinner."

"What, nothing about the company?"

"Well, that goes without saying."

Sarah grinned across the table. "Yeah, Ernie, I know a lot of things go without saying. It's funny about you and me. Sometimes we think things we don't say. Sometimes we say things without thinking and wish we hadn't. Guess it happens to everybody."

They'd been talking about lots of subjects during dinner—the investigation, the paper, their families, and eventually how they'd met in McKinney's class a decade ago. "Did you ever imagine you'd be saying something like 'a decade ago,' Ernie? A decade seemed like half a lifetime when you were in school, which in fact it was. Now time goes by so fast you just don't want to waste a single minute of it."

No, I don't, Ernie thought. and I wish I knew how to avoid doing it. I wish—what he was wishing for just then was making his blood race. He was acutely conscious of this beautiful girl in this beautiful body. It was dark, and still quite warm. "C'mon," Sarah said, standing and walking around the table to Ernie. "We're going for a walk."

Sarah knew she'd been saying "C'mon" to Ernie all evening, and wondered if that telegraphed her intentions, hoping so. She took his hand and led him out the door. They walked around the house and down the lane, past the mailbox where she used to wait for the schoolbus with Elena. They turned right and headed up the road past the fields. The moon was high now, not full, but bright. No manmade lights were in sight, or needed. A half mile past Elena's house Sarah turned them onto a small path and headed toward the spring, one of several subterranean fountains that filled a lake the size of a foot-ball field. The spring had produced without interruption since the beginning of time, or so the legend ran, and Papa Beto had generously shared its bounty with his neighbors.

For as long as Sarah could remember, the lake had overflowed at the same place, in the same measure, spilling into a kind of eternal stream, where underwater grasses nearly a yard long danced in the current. One day years earlier, she and Elena had discovered a secret—at the edge of the stream, far enough from the trees to al-ways be in sunlight, a shallow pocket had formed where the water stilled, and on cloudless days warmed to near bath temperature. It held the heat for hours, a natural, grass-lined spa. A log was lying by the spring. Sarah sat on it and removed her shoes.

"C'mon, Ernie, take off yours."

He felt another jolt, and really didn't mind. Being traditional, his shoes had laces. He untied them, removed his shoes and socks, and when he looked up, Sarah was standing ankle-deep in the water, about ten feet in front of him. It couldn't have been planned, but the moon was behind her, highlighting her hair and shoulders, framing her body through her dress with light that bounced off the gentle ripples on the pond. He gasped.

"You're a vision."

He thought she smiled at that, but it was hard to see in the moon shadow.

"Do you really think so, Ernest Hemmingway?"

"Sarah, you're the most beautiful vision I've ever seen."

"Really?"

"Yes."

"Honest?" He skipped a beat.

"About as honest, I think, as I could ever be."

"Okay."

Then, as he sat there looking at her, she reached down to the hem of her dress and lifted it up over her body, stretching her arms above her until her dress was free.

195

She tossed it onto the grass. "Still a vision, Ernie?"

He nearly choked. After a minute, which he would re-live a great many times, he realized she wore nothing under her dress.

"Now, my gentleman friend from Montego Bay, you and I are going skinny dipping in the Caribbean." She turned, ran three steps, and dived cleanly into the water. He was aching for this girl now, not only for the body shown him, but for all of her. Was there anyone else with a spirit like hers, a magic like hers? He doubted it. He was in the water quickly, but she was already near the other side of the lake. He was a good swimmer, had prac-tically lived in the ocean growing up in Jamaica, and hap-pily struck out after her. But when he was halfway across the pond he realized she had swum to the side.

Ah, Marco Polo tag, is it? He changed course, watch-ing her now, but it was a good five minutes before he caught her, and when he did, she wrapped her arms around him and kissed him passionately, pressing against him, arms and legs encircling him. Then she just held on to him. "My darling," she whispered.

She broke away then and swam to the outflow and he followed her. Water ran across the natural spillway nearly six inches deep. She sat up on the edge, again making him gasp, then turned and slid down on the grasses be-yond. He did the same and moments later, to his amaze-ment, found himself in a sweet smelling grass-pillowed bed of warmth. It was scarcely more than a foot in depth.

They lay there together for a time, their heads on the gentle slope at the side, and then Sarah said, "You realize, Ernie, that this was the plan. I'm going on record here, not quite public but definitely on record, that I'm seducing you. I wanted to make love to you the night you walked me home for three hours in college, but you were too shy and I was too proud. I'd said all my life I wouldn't start it with anyone, because that meant I'd be beholden. So I'm on record right now that I'm prepared to be beholden to you for the rest of my life, and if you'd please ask me if I will marry you, I will say yes."

"Will you–?"

"Yes!" she shouted, and rolled onto him and kissed him. Then it was urgent and tender and then slower and more tender and there, in the moonlight, he knew his heart would be linked with hers for the rest of time. There were a million stars in the sky that night. He counted them.

* * * *

Thanks to Willy Carlson's legal expertise, Sarah's divorce proceedings moved swiftly. Carlson also counseled her to file an embezzlement suit against her husband. Following a preliminary hearing, Martin was arraigned, his car impounded, and a trial in Keaton County criminal court scheduled for six weeks later.

Just days after his expulsion from Oak Hills, Daniels had found work as an accountant for a small film company. His employer appreciated his creativity with the books, and Martin appreciated finding an easy access to cocaine, which he now increasingly craved.

The company made adult movies, mostly on location in Palm Springs, where it rented a comfortable house with a Spanish-arched courtyard two blocks north of Palm Canyon Drive. A discreet film crew and an eight-foot bougainvillea-covered wall around the yard and pool assured privacy; neighbors had no idea anyone was filming next door. It also meant that the company could by-pass business licenses and commercial zoning ordinances. Martin worked at the producer's office in West Hollywood, a ten minute walk from his small studio apartment. His addiction had now coiled around him like a boa constrictor, and his thinking centered around drugs most of the time. The need for cash was constant, with *The Echo* money long gone. Now his car had been taken away as well.

"Okay," he mused, "so I don't have wheels. What the hell. I know where I can get a car, and even if I don't really need it, it'll get me some cash. I'll just hop a bus up to Oak Hills, drive Sarah's back to Nicky's place in Studio City, and he can hock it down in Tijuana. Her Plymouth will be a nice little limo down there. A few hundred is just what I need right now. There's no way she'll remember I've still got a key."

Work at the *The Echo* continued apace, with the day-to-day gathering of birth, death, legal, civic, sport, farm and business news. The bottling company would soon expand, and bring new employment. Quality of life had surfaced as the big issue, with money, as always, the catalyst—in whose hands would it eventually end up? That would be the front page story for tomorrow's edition.

As had been the practice at the paper for years, Sarah planned to leave the the final editorial copy on her desk for the typesetter, who would come in to work at 4:00 a.m. This issue about growth had important ramifications for everyone in Oak Hills. With effort, Sarah disassociated herself from her personal affairs and the Caulfield investigation to concentrate on the story. But she knew it would be another late night.

* * * *

Bull Haymore felt a high as he walked out of the ranch house on the butte above Little Sequoia. He'd had a hard day in the field and a good steak dinner. And now he was a man with a mission. The mission was neither rational, nor thought-through, nor prudent, but Haymore was never big on those kinds of considerations. Tonight he had a job to do, and he'd looked forward to it ever since that bitch got away in the canyon. He topped off his gas tank from the gravity feed by the tractor shed and checked his oil. His truck was running smoothly. Ten minutes later he was headed down the Rattlesnake toward Oak Hills. On the floor of the passenger side was a cooler full of ice and longneck beers. He'd thought ahead

that much. This was the Thursday night he'd been planning for and his mission would require a little patience.
On the seat beside him was the 12-gauge shotgun he used
to knock birds out of the sky, vermin out of their holes,
and occasionally a coyote out of the hen house. Yes sir,
he was prepared. Just imagining what he was going to do
made him hard.

"Sometimes you just gotta take care of things personally," Bull said aloud, to no one but himself. "When you
gotta do somethin' you gotta do it. How did that bitch
find out about me? Jesus, I been workin' up here for 14
years and nothin' like this ever happened." He opened a
beer.

"We kept the kid ever since he went off his rocker and
nobody ever knew. So how'd she find out? Shit, he was
as good as dead the whole time anyway. All we had to do
was keep him on the ranch. And with TV to watch, that's
all it took. Course now I'm just another hand. Two years
o' shit work but Russell still pays me somethin' at least.
Mostly for nothin,' really, just jerkin' off 'til I can get
down with Annie. Now there's a bitch. The bitch in the
greenhouse shoulda been like her, ready and able. Those
fuckin' Keaton Pansies shit right there in their pants, they
did. Took Garth and me to tell 'em what to do."

It was time for another beer. Every few minutes Bull
flicked on his off-road lights, which illumined the canyon
like mid-day. Yeah, they're working fine, and they'll
work tonight.

"Jesus, Russell found Garth fast. Just about killed him. Never saw a guy beat up so bad. Yeah, Russell's one mean sonofabitch. Got the story outa Garth quick, he did. Course that's how come I got this job. I coulda got smashed up, too. Now this bitch stickin' her nose where it don't belong, that's no good for me. Gotta take care of that."

* * * *

Sarah wrote the last paragraph of the story. It was a quote from the final speaker at the public hearing on the zoning change for the bottling plant. Emily Karchner, the alert and involved 80-year old pioneer mother of Oak Hills' famous World War II hero, had said little but had said a lot. Her eldest son had died in 1942 saving the lives of half his platoon on Bataan. She had three children, seven grandchildren and seven great-grandchildren.

"I welcome the opportunity the new plant will bring for my children and their children," Emily had begun. "Lord knows we need all the opportunity we can get. But people, I don't welcome some of the things that seem to come with what we like to call 'growth.' Read the papers from Los Angeles, even San Jose. Do we want that kind of crime and violence here? And just what do we mean by growth, anyway? Is getting bigger growth? Are we taller? Or just fatter?

"My husband and I came here when there were less than a hundred souls living in what is our Oak Hills today. We made a life here and it was a good one. It still is. But to get these 300 new jobs will the 3,000 souls who live here today sacrifice what they came for in the first place? That's the real question now."

Sarah left the story on her desk with a note for the typesetter, turned out the light in her office and put her coffee cup in the sink. I'll wash it in the morning, she thought, wearily heading for the door. She brushed back a strand of hair from her forehead. How she missed Ernie! He'd be home tomorrow, back in her arms, and hadn't left her heart for a moment.

It had rained lightly, and the air was fragrant with the smell of moisture on the dry hills. We needed this, she said under her breath, turning to put her key in the lock. Then she faintly heard a motor and turned to see a vehicle slowly moving toward the street. It was running without lights. Her car!

"Stop!" she screamed, racing toward the gravel drive that led to the street. Suddenly, just as the car reached the road, it was flooded with a blaze of light from the bushes on the other side. Almost at the same instant, shots shattered the night. Sarah stopped as if she had run into a stone wall. Nothing seemed to compute. Then she heard the roar of a powerful motor and the squeal of tires.

She raced back into the office and called the sheriff. The dispatcher answered on the first ring, heard her story, the fear in her voice, and told her a deputy would be on the scene in less than five minutes. She also ordered her to lock all her doors, turn out the lights and stay inside.

Still dazed and unbelieving, the darkness of the room only increased Sarah's terror. Despite the warning, she picked up a small flashlight from the shelf by the entrance, opened the door and stepped outside.

There was no sound. Only silence that quivered her bones. Compelled as if by a puppeteer, she moved toward the road. When she reached it, she could see her car straddling the narrow drive. The back window was shattered, partly gone. Slowly she stepped along the left of the vehicle, keeping as far away as the bushes allowed. First she saw the windshield was gone. Then she realized the driver's head was gone as well, literally blown to pieces, splattered throughout the interior. She turned away, retching, and somehow found her way back to the office door. At that moment a spotlight encircled her, and she heard, "Stop right there! Put your hands up!"

Ten seconds later she was on the ground, face down, her wrists being twisted behind her to be cuffed.

In spite of her protestations and some language she never knew she knew, she was put into the back seat of the police cruiser by a very nervous young officer who had never been called to a crime scene before, and who insisted that the person who reported the incident was still in the building. Minutes later the watch commander arrived and immediately recognized her.

"God almighty, Sarah, first it was that road chase up on the Rattlesnake, and now this. You into drugs or something?" It was hours before she learned that the driver of her car had been Martin, and hours more before the shock of the revelation let her speak without her throat closing. He had been the worst kind of husband, who'd lied, cheated, stolen, taken her to ecstasy in his arms; but she had loved him in her ignorance, and now seen the bloody end of it all with his head blown into a million pieces.

The detectives put the events together quickly. Armed with warrants, they descended on the Russell ranch in Little Sequoia before noon the next day. They found the pickup, with tires that matched the tracks left across the road from *The Echo* office. Haymore's shotgun, now carefully cleaned, was also taken as evidence. They arrested Haymore as the suspect in Martin's murder. Ex-sheriff Russell claimed he knew nothing about either the road chase or the shooting.

"Hell, you guys, I have no idea of a motive. The fucker's just a ranch hand."

"The ranch hand is also a fuckin' idiot," Russell mumbled to himself as the detectives took Bull away in cuffs. "I should have dumped him when the kid died, but who would'a thought he could ever have been this stupid? Jesus, he'd actually tried to run the Baker woman off the Rattlesnake! Moron!"

Russell had figured it made sense to bring Bull Haymore to the ranch after Timmy Caulfield came back from the Connecticut hospital as a vegetable. Bull wanted to keep the lid on more than anybody, he thought, and he was sure as hell cheap labor. But such a halfwit! Now he's killed a guy. If Caulfield were alive he would'a pissed in his pants.

The thought made Russell look to the west, to the JKC ranch, where the landing strip at the edge of the property, once carefully trimmed and leveled, was now knee high with grass. "Just lucky Bull never screwed up in front of the old man. Of course 'bout all he had to do was get Timmy ready for the flights. Goin' up with his dad in that little plane was the only jollies the kid ever got. Caulfield came to see him so regular we shoulda had him delivering milk."

* * * *

Oh Sarah," Ernie exclaimed, aghast at the story she poured out the moment he walked in the door of *The Echo*. "Thank God you're okay. What was Martin doing in your car? And in the middle of the night? Was he trying to steal it? I doubt if he was the real target."

"But who was then?"

"I think you were."

"Ernie!" she cried. "Why me?"

"Because Haymore was one of the killers of Ursula Ketterman. The Annie you talked with in Little Sequoia last month must have tipped him off. Otherwise he could never have moved fast enough to follow you down the mountain. He'll get what's coming to him for killing

Martin, even if we don't have anything but hearsay evidence that he was connected with Ursula's murder."

"What about Russell then? Haymore was working on his ranch."

"Russell's a rat, but he's probably kept within the law. So he's a legal rat."

* * * *

Sarah and Ernie finalized their plan on Tuesday. It would involve special printing, creative script writing, and play acting that might qualify them for an Oscar–if they could stay out of jail. They would risk their careers as journalists, through a publication they were creating out of thin air, to learn and expose the truth, with all of its tentacles, about the murder of Ursula Ketterman. At midnight on the following Friday, a determined, if anxious, young woman caught the redeye to New York. Sleep had been of secondary interest for some time. On the flight she slept all the way.

PART EIGHT

Monday morning, Miss Sarah Baker, ostensibly a writer for the audacious, ambitious, and to date, unknown, *Mind and Body* Magazine, walked into the medical library of Columbia University School of Medicine in New York City. Her newly minted partner in crime, an expert researcher since his student days at Northwestern, had carefully coached her in how to ferret out the latest information on psychiatry, and find details going back 30 years on celebrated cases involving lobotomies. Ernie knew three cases would be in the medical literature because they'd been in the mass media first.

Two involved prisoners serving life sentences in states that had no death penalty: one inmate had hacked five coeds to death on a grisly night and pledged to repeat it each school year; the other claimed he had been told by the devil, whom he worshiped, that his role in life was to judge every judge with a bullet in his brain so there would be more justice in hell. The third case involved the son of a wealthy New England family who had mutilated himself to the point of death. He had used scissors, doors that he could close on his hands or feet, or any other means of inflicting pain and trauma upon himself. Of course the treatment of the third case was to have been conducted in the utmost confidentiality. Yet Ernie had read about it in the popular press, led off by the *London*

Daily Mirror, which reported in three-inch headlines that the parents of Jonathan Erskin IV had committed their 26-year-old son and heir to Connecticut's Rose Hills Institute, a secret resource of the rich and famous in America for dealing with impossible family members and possible enemies. Enterprising English reporters had somehow found a hole in the dike of professional discretion at the Institute, and presented the case history of the boy in merciless detail, complete with photographs of the institute taken from the air, and school photographs of poor little mentally unbalanced Jonathan, with Ivy League hair style and open collar and sweater. There were no photographs after age 14. Only subsequently did the case reach medical literature, in a reasoned case analysis in the venerable *New England Journal of Medicine*, a publication not given to discussing the quackery of the "medicine" conducted in the popular press. Due to the celebrity of the event and in defense of the Hippocratic calling, the editor himself had felt compelled to address the science and medical ethics involved.

Another case caught Sarah's attention. In the Fall 1941 issue of "Physician's Report," newsletter of the Boston Psychiatric Hospital, she read that a daughter of Mr. Joseph Kennedy had been admitted to Rose Hills institute in Connecticut for treatment. No further information was given. Returning to what she'd come for, Sarah probed into the subject of commitment authorization, examining its legal, moral and religious implications. She noted key phrases, scientific terminology, physician conclusions and case reports, and copied the details to keep and commit to memory.

Under the category *Hospitals, Psychiatric*, Sarah looked up Rose Hills, extracting two names, one the hospital's Director of Communications, the other its Head Physician. In *Who's Who?* She learned their histories, including a sad episode in the family of the Director. Those people held the positions Ernie had advised her to select, even though he hadn't known who they were. Then she discovered an item she had not searched for, but realized could be significant; the entry in Rose Hills financial records of a $50,000 endowment to the Institute for ongoing support of a surgical internship. The grant, made in November, 1942 was from the Chairman of the Board of Caulfield Communications, Tigh Harbor, California, J. Kenneth Caulfield. If Ernie's supposition was correct, November, 1942 was near one month after Timothy Caulfield was turned into a garden-variety vegetable by a Rose Hills surgeon's knife.

My God, what kind of a father would do that to his son? Could he possibly have imagined it as an act of mercy? The boy was disturbed, certainly, had been at the vortex of the maelstrom surrounding the murder of Ursula Ketterman. But did Caulfield have him cut for the boy's sake or his own? Might it really have been to ensure that no scandal could emerge one day to stain the Caulfield legacy? Could they ever prove anything?

She and Ernie had formed a plan and set out to implement it. She'd been certain at that time they could pull it off, and was equally uncertain now. The plan was audacious, but so risky, so dependent on gullibility, luck, and the alignment of the stars, it beggared the odds. Ernie was no stranger to self doubt, had enough for both of them, yet neither had taken risks like they were proposing now. Their options had narrowed down to one: a make-believe magazine called *Mind and Body,* which just might reveal the secrets of Old Doc Milosovic.

Old Doc had delivered Timothy Caulfield to the plane in California for the flight to Connecticut. If the boy's commitment was legal, a licensed physician had to have been involved. But Old Doc had sold his practice years before. Did he still have a license? Was there another doctor? If not, the commitment was a felony. The general public would consider it an atrocious act, involving not only a physician but the prominent father of a victimized patient. What a scandal for smug little Tigh Harbor! The only problem with that is that anyone who could be indicted is dead and gone.

Except for Rose Hills!

Might the good folks at Rose Hills Institute have been so excited about receiving an endowment they failed to verify the legitimacy of the doctor who committed a teenage boy to undergo a lobotomy? Of course if Ernie and I get the evidence illegally it would never stand up in court. But would it ever get to court?

Sarah, here you are playing private eye without a license, being highly creative with the truth, and putting together a risky, dangerous sting. And whether it's successful or not, could Rose Hills sue us? For everything? What's our everything? It would hardly be worth the effort for them to mount a lawsuit to get all we've got; Martin took care of that. And there would be smelly publicity if Rose Hills' dirty linen got aired in public. So is there an outside chance that the Institute would be desperate enough to keep a terrible mistake under wraps that they'd be blackmailable? Sarah, Sarah, what have you come to? Well—this.

Frank McGee

PART NINE

On Wednesday morning, at 11:20 Eastern Standard time, Creighton L. Bingham, Director of Development and Public affairs of the Rose Hills Institute in Greenwich, Connecticut, was sitting at his desk in a Brooks Brothers suit sipping Earl Grey tea from a Limoges cup when he received a call from Ernest M. Hemmingway, Publisher and Editor in Chief of *Mind and Body Magazine*. After introducing himself as if it were unnecessary, really, Hemmingway informed Mr. Bingham in somewhat grandiloquent prose that the Scientific Advisory Board of "this ground-breaking new publication" had proposed Rose Hills Institute as the cover story of the magazine's inaugural issue. The focus would be on the latest developments in psychiatric care. "That focus, I must assure you, Dr. Bingham, is now of priority interest to Dr. Leroy Burney, Surgeon General of the United States."

Bingham carefully placed the cup in its saucer, slid it to the side of his antique walnut desk, and reached for his gold plated pen.

"Well, Mr...uh, Hemmingway, that's very interesting. Tell me more, if you will, so I can have a better—"

"The publication date of *Mind and Body's* first issue is

still three months away, Dr. Bingham," Ernie continued with scarcely a breath, "but I can assure you, sir, our editorial offices are running full steam ahead, as if the deadline is tomorrow! You understand what I mean—there are just *so* many aspects to cover. Actually there are deadlines pretty much every day now. Oh, yes, and of course the manuscript and photos will all be subject to your review. Professional courtesy, you know."

"Of course, Mr. Hemmingway. Such oversight is essential in any material published about Rose Hills Institute. We are not Bellevue or Mayo here you know." Bingham, a much traveled man, tried to identify the accent of the caller. *Mind & Body. Hemmingway. Burney. Review.* He had notes.

"Certainly, and of course we respect that completely, Dr. Bingham. That's why we're so excited about the content of our premier issue. I'm sure you've been following the birth of this literary 'newborn,'" Ernie continued, "but as these are still early days you may not be aware that we're underwritten by endowments from the selfsame foundations that provide the majority of funds flowing to private hospitals." Ernie took a deep breath and chuckled softly, giving Bingham a chance to comment. Prudently, he did not; he'd never heard of *Mind and Body*.

"Well, Mr. Bingham, our features editor, Miss Sarah Baker–a remarkable young woman I must say–is in Washington at the moment with the Surgeon General, but

I've instructed her to get together with you as soon as possible. Might you be able to carve out, say, an hour or so on Friday afternoon, day after tomorrow, for her to drop by for an initial discussion on how we might best proceed?

"You'll enjoy her, Dr. Bingham, I assure you; She's from the West Coast publishing family and was the star journalism graduate at Northwestern. Is without doubt the most gifted writer we have seen (we interviewed 35 others, but worked very hard to bring her aboard, such a delight!) and, oh yes, we're sending you complete information about the genesis and launch of *Mind and Body*. Very exciting, like nothing else in the field. The collateral material is due back from the printer on Friday, and I'll have it overnighted to you. I must say it's one deadline after another around here these days you know, but of course you deal with that sort of thing all the time, don't you, Dr. Bingham, representing Rose Hills as you do to the whole world?"

Such an obsequious observation obviously required no answer, and Ernie didn't pause for one. "You'll note in the announcement that we're printing 150,000 copies of our first edition, establishing us as the most widely-read medical periodical in the country. But that's just our initial edition, of course, which will be quite a collector's item. We'll publish quarterly. The second edition will simmer down to a conservative 100,000! Rather exciting, wouldn't you say?"

Bingham, more confounded than excited by the numbers, mumbled an indecipherable response.

"Distribution," Ernie continued, "is via first class mail, and fully ninety percent of the recipients will be health care professionals. The other ten percent will be the country's thought leaders, which is what seems to have caught the Surgeon General's attention, considering that the *New England Journal* is basically for physicians; Dr. Burney is such a strategist in understanding how to influence public opinion in the most positive ways.

"Well thank you, Dr. Bingham, and I know you'll enjoy Miss Baker, and do call me if you have any questions about anything, just anything at all. We're frightfully into these early deadlines right now, as I said, but I'll make sure to get back to you the very soonest if you aren't able to reach me on the first try. Cheerio, Dr. Bingham."

Ernie hung up and stared at the phone, barely believing what he had just done. A few minutes later he picked the phone up again and called GTE to arrange for a Carmel number to be call-forwarded to the new phone in his apartment above *The Echo*. Then he went downtown to buy one of the new wire recorder telephone answering machines.

* * * *

The buff-colored parchment calling card had a formal look. Mind and Body was centered in the middle in gold foil caps. The magazine's ephemeral Carmel, California address was in raised brown Garamond type, with the editorial office telephone listed below it. The name at the bottom was Sarah Baker, Features Editor. Thus armed, on Friday afternoon punctually at 2:30, Sarah arrived at the heavy wrought-iron gate of the Rose Hills institute. A guard approached.

"Good afternoon, officer. I am Sarah Baker and Mr. Bingham is expecting me." The gate swung back and Sarah drove up the quarter mile entryway into what could have been a movie set. Enormous colonnades framed the hospital portico. Gnarled old vines wound up the white stone walls, weaving a tapestry begun - how many decades earlier? There were acres of rolling lawns, immense old trees with benches under them, idyllic settings for quiet talks.

Awestruck, Sarah gave herself a slap back to the business at hand with the thought, yeah, nice places to talk to a patient before you hand him over to some orderly and go back to your office or your mistress or your bar. At the moment, Sarah's challenge was to make herself appear credible and her assignment legitimate. If she could do that, she might be able to pull off a hit-and-run today. This is the game to win, Sarah. There won't be another one.

"Good afternoon, Miss Baker."

She was startled to hear a voice like Ernie's. The man stepping from behind his desk to greet her in the sunny, finely-furnished office, had the demeanor and dress of an English gentleman. But of course this was Ivy League country.

"Dr. Bingham, it's good of you to see me at such short notice."

"That was no problem."

"And now, it seems, notices are getting shorter still. At the Sheraton when I checked in there was a message to call Washington again. I've just come from there."

"Ah, yes, Mr. Hemmingway told me you were interviewing the Surgeon General. An excellent man, Dr. Burney, very well qualified." He motioned Sarah to an overstuffed leather chair. "Coffee?"

"Thank you. Just a touch of cream, if you please. Of course our connection with the Surgeon General isn't to be made public yet, but I know Mr. Hemmingway wants you to be aware of all that's happening. After all, Dr. Burney will be featured in the issue together with the Institute. That's what the call from Washington was about, in fact. It seems I'm expected to meet with Dr. Burney at six tomorrow in Georgetown. Something of a command performance, it sounded like. But he's a very engaging personality, and how do you say no to someone like that?"

Sarah accepted the cup, took a sip and then stood, moving to the oak paneled wall alongside Bingham's desk. It was minimally adorned. Three framed certificates hung there, one a Masters degree in business administration from Princeton, one a Bachelors from New York State, the other an illuminated honorary award from the American Psychiatry Association. Saying nothing, Sarah read every word of the third certificate, then turned to look at Bingham.

"I know it's true," Sarah said. "You've made an enormous contribution. I hope we'll be able to do that justice in our inaugural edition. In fact, Dr. Burney told me yesterday he wants to make certain of it. You've been central to so much of the progress that's been made."

Bingham coughed modestly. "Well, *Mind and Body* certainly seems to be getting off to a fast start, doesn't it?"

"It does indeed, Dr. Bingham," Sarah continued as she moved back to the chair. "Incidentally, Dr. Burney reiterated on the phone this afternoon the suggestion he made to me yesterday, that when the issue is finalized, he wanted to meet in Washington with Mr. Hemmingway, you, and Dr. McKenzie. I had no idea, really, that he would respond as he has to the intent of this feature. He's not only a physician but a visionary."

Sarah paused, looked out the window across the lawns, and drew what she hoped might approximate an oratorical breath. Bingham quietly nodded his head, reached for his cup and slowly, briefly, stirred its contents. He sat back and waited for Sarah to continue, apparently feeling no compulsion to inject his own thoughts into the conversation. Sarah realized that here was a man who naturally possessed social skills that few attain. She looked at him and smiled.

"Our conversations with Dr. Burney over these past weeks left me with a mixture of emotions, I must admit," Sarah said, pausing to allow a moment for comment, which was not forthcoming. "At times I was puzzled, at times distressed, at times euphoric. I've never met anyone with a wider horizon, or a more empathetic approach to what people need now and will need to prepare for in times to come. He has been looking at the possibility of viruses from some animals in Africa migrating to humans, of infections becoming so resistant to the overuse of antibiotics that existing antibiotics stop being effective at all. Many more issues are on his list of daily concerns."

Another pause. Then Sarah continued.

"But when he heard of a subject we planned to focus on next year, he urged us to move it up and make it the feature of our inaugural, to deal with it right now! In essence, it is the need lift the psychological cloud that is building over the people of this country. The causes are many, from political and economic to personal. When Dr. Burney learned we were considering it at all, he very strongly advised us, twisted our arms really, to launch the magazine with it. He sees our premiere issue as the ideal platform through which to prepare the country for a major campaign he's planning to launch along those lines. I must say, he's a strategist."

"Well, *Mind and Body* will obviously be treating vital issues."

"Yes indeed, but Dr. Burney jumped about a year ahead of us, saw us as a kind of springboard. I had known the costs of treating mental illness were enormous, but frankly I was astounded when he told me that currently there are well over half a million psychiatric patients in U.S. hospitals. I'm not sure how to relate to that figure—a seemingly incredible statement! I hope you can help me here, Doctor. We'll need unassailable evidence if we're to give it our editorial imprimatur. But I've certainly become aware, as I've examined the issue, of the uneasiness, the undercurrent of angst beneath the prosperity so many enjoy. People fear the bubble will burst, that they could experience again the tragic times of the great depression, and that the almighty Atom that ended the war could some day end all of civilization. So two kinds of depression loom, threatening our mental health as well as our economy."

Sarah realized she sounded like someone reading a seminar paper. She changed the pace.

"Of course I'm not speaking as a physician here, or a scientist. Just a writer. But this issue has assumed a compelling urgency for all of us at the magazine. And time, unfortunately, is not on our side. Obviously I'll now need to leave for Washington by noon tomorrow, but for a very brief period there, I'm certain. I wonder if you could visit with me on Monday for, perhaps, two or three hours?

And I would like to have time with Dr. McKenzie also, if it could be arranged."

"I see no problem with that, Miss Baker. Dr. McKenzie will return from Boston Sunday. He's being honored there tomorrow by the American Psychiatric Association. For fifty years he's been a pioneer in the profession."

"A very distinguished career, which I'm sure has added greatly to the reputation of Rose Hills. But I'm also aware of how vitally important you have been to the institute, Dr. Bingham. More important, I suspect, than most people realize."

"Well, I've been here for a time, Miss Baker, and I wouldn't characterize myself as important, but I do care rather deeply about our people and our mission, and want to see it represented as it really is."

"Exactly, Dr. Bingham, and we'll certainly be able to do that in the feature. We want to show the great advances in research and treatment, and the hospital's part in that. Dr. Burney told me how you came to be so faithfully dedicated to this objective. I had no idea you and your brother had experienced such a tragedy. That ennobles your work even more"

"What? I was not aware Dr. Burney knew of my family's misfortune. Really, I—"

"Dr. Bingham, I think that's one of the reasons he wants to meet with you and Dr. McKenzie. His concern is for real people and real lives, not for statistics. What happened to your mother, I must tell you, was one of the key factors that decided him to place the focus of his office on the mental health of the nation."

Bingham brought his cup halfway to his lips and held it there, staring into it, seeing something other than coffee. His face was less impassive now, less Ivy League.

Sarah waited for some moments before she spoke.

"To develop this feature most effectively, Dr. Bingham, we'll want to contrast the psychiatric practice of the thirties, when surgery was introduced as treatment, to the therapies of today."

"But surely, Miss Baker, that therapy is not an issue anymore, not with the drugs available now."

"Exactly the point, Dr. Bingham. The only reason even to refer to it is to show how far we've come. It's like starting with the horse and buggy in an article about the auto industry. If you'll allow me, here's what I'd like to accomplish in the brief time we have right now. I realize that with tomorrow being Saturday, your staff may be reduced. Depending on the time available before I have to leave for Washington, I wondered if I might assess whatever you could show me about the institute's founding, the initial endowment structure, the norms of medicine at the time, and of course the growth and physical additions over the years. Would that be possible? Then on Monday, there are three cases I would appreciate discussing with you, though only one was related to the Institute. Hopefully they'll help us put all the advances in perspective."

"Miss Baker, with respect, none of our cases can be discussed. Discretion is an absolute at Rose Hills."

"Oh, of course, Dr. Bingham, and we honor that. These cases have all been in the media. What I'm hoping to talk about are the differences in how they might have been dealt with today. And of course we can credit the information to our own research in any case. There need be no attribution at all."

Bingham still looked uncomfortable, but said nothing.

"Two of the cases were in the forties," Sarah continued, "involving persons incarcerated for serious crimes, one in Washington State, one in Indiana. You may be aware of them, because they had wide media coverage, although of course that was long before your time."

"Well, not really, although—"

"The ripples were in the press for at least a decade. The third was the case of the Erskin boy, and I'm sure Dr. McKenzie will have interesting perspectives on that after so many years. A few comments on these cases will take us quickly into the real thrust of the feature, which is the hope now on the horizon for persons suffering in torment under the anxieties and contradictions of modern life. Regarding our schedule, might it be possible for you to show me a little of the facility still today? The physical setting is superb here, Dr. Bingham, quite without equal."

"You should note that I'm usually addressed as *Mr.* Bingham here, young lady, as my doctorate is in Administration; but you're very kind. Let's have a bite to eat first and then we can take a brief tour. Supper here is rather early."

It was good. Evidently anyone who could afford the services of Rose Hills could afford a gourmet kitchen. Sarah realized that in the chaos of the last weeks she'd neglected not only fine dining but sometimes dining at all. And Bingham was pleasant company. So far, she calculated, she'd been accepted at face value, although her current face was false. She felt a genuine sympathy for her host, knowing from her research at Columbia what had happened to his mother. But she left that subject alone. Instead, the Bingham name was the topic. Yes, her host's great uncle had been the Bingham who discovered the ancient Machu Picchu ruins in the Peruvian Andes. Yes, he'd been to see them. How strong those people must have been, living at that altitude. Visiting the site left you breathless, in more ways than one.

On the tour after supper Sarah asked about the Rose Hills records of the past 100 years, commenting that they must be voluminous.

"Yes, they're nearly all on microfiche now, all in a machine not much bigger than my desk. We're keeping the originals, of course. they're historic documents, even if no one will ever see them. Our records center is probably the largest room in the hospital. All temperature and humidity controlled. One of our biggest tasks when we began doing this was to cross-reference every patient profile, diagnosis and treatment. Twelve technicians worked on that task for 18 months. It has provided us with a uniquely valuable research databank."

Sarah worked to keep her expression impassive, to hide the fact that her stomach had done a flip. Bingham had just described the motherlode!

"Now that's simply extraordinary," she enthused. "Amazing! Everything by date, symptom, response, history? What a monumental achievement!"

"We're very proud of this, Miss Baker. There's nothing like it anywhere."

"And *that's it*, Dr.–I mean Mr. Bingham!" Sarah exclaimed suddenly, grinning from ear to ear. "You've just pointed me to the element I've been searching for, the perfect lead for the feature. Imagine being in that room, surrounded by the hopes and heartaches of hundreds of human beings. It would be an emotional connection that the reader simply couldn't ignore. Can we go there?"

"Miss Baker, that is our holy of holies. I'm sure you're aware of that. But yes, we can take a brief look at it, and if you want to write something about your impression of it, of course that would be fine."

It was a vast room in the basement, filled with vintage oak filing cabinets. Bingham explained how it was organized. "Here are the 20s, the 30s, the 40s, etc. Patients are listed by name. In those indexes over there they are cross-listed by name, diagnosis and treatment."

"Unbelievable!" Sarah exclaimed. "This is just what I had been hoping existed. I want to absorb the history of this room, use it as the foundation for the whole article. Can I take a little time here to allow the magnitude of this place to impinge? This room is surely going to introduce our premiere edition."

"I really must close the week's reports before leaving this evening, Miss Baker, and I'm sorry, I'm just not able to stay." For a moment that to Sarah seemed endless, Bingham looked into the imploring face of his visitor.

"But perhaps our security chief could be with you here. You understand why that is necessary, of course."

"Oh, certainly."

Bingham went to the phone on the wall and dialed a number.

"John? Where's John? Oh. Well, Fred, would you please come to the Records Room to be with Miss Sarah Baker? She's doing research for a medical feature and unfortunately I have to leave. She shouldn't need more than twenty more minutes here." He glanced at his visitor as she nodded. "Thank you."

Turning back to Sarah, he said, "He'll be here in a moment. Tomorrow I'll be in my office at 8:00 a.m., and we can— "

"Thank you for all your courtesy, Mr. Bingham. I'll just sit outside here until he comes.

As soon as Bingham left, Sarah moved quickly back into the Records Room. In the filing cabinet labeled 1940-45 she searched for Caulfield, willing her inner butterflies that if they must fly like this, damn it, get in formation. In the middle of the "C" drawer she found the folder. Inside there were several documents and records. With shaking hands, she photographed them one by one under the harsh fluorescents with her half-frame Minox camera, which was loaded with high-speed Kodak film. Just as she put the camera away, she turned to find the guard standing at the door, watching her. Her heart froze.

"Hello," she heard a voice say, "you must be Fred." She realized the words had just come out of her own mouth, and instantly continued. "What an amazing place this is, Fred, with everything for a hundred years at your fingertips. What a resource! Have you been at Rose Hills for a long time, Fred? Oh yes, by the way, I'm Sarah Baker." Her most dazzling smile.

"We're preparing a landmark medical feature for *Mind and Body* magazine together with Dr. Burney, the U.S. Surgeon General. We'll be focusing on Rose Hills and the state of the art in psychiatric medicine. You can be so proud of being part of this, Fred. Oh, you're with Pinkerton? Well, that's been the very best security company for more than a century, isn't that right?"

As she was speaking, Sarah casually placed the documents back into their folder, then returned it to its proper place in the drawer. She moved to an adjacent cabinet, opened it, picked a file, removed a document.

"Brilliant." She moved to another.

"What year were you born, Fred? 1931? Well, let's see."

Sarah quickly found the 1930s, opened a drawer and took out a folder.

"Isn't this astounding, Fred? Just look at this. Right here are stories of families your parents might have known. When you and I were still just a twinkle in our daddy's eyes, there were dedicated people caring for the needs of everyone who lived, and we can scarcely imagine now how they could do it so well with the limited knowledge and resources they had then. Well, that's pretty much what I need. Do you work all night? Midnight? Wow, that's almost an emergency room doctor's schedule. Well, it takes a great many professionals to make all this work, doesn't it?"

From a pay phone ten miles away, Sarah called Ernie, unable to disguise her elation.

"Sarah, that's wonderful. you'll win an Oscar for sure. When Bingham realizes . . ."

"And the guard just stood there and talked about his family and . . ."

Ernie's even demeanor soon brought Sarah back to

earth, and she commanded herself to stop counting her chickens, or anything else. She drove to La Guardia, and caught the midnight United Airlines redeye to San Francisco. There, she picked up her car and drove the 185 miles to Oak Hills, stopping once for coffee and to relieve her protesting bladder.

The film was processed by three p.m. Sarah and Ernie hovered anxiously over the developing table as the photos began to come visible in the chemical bath. Once they determined that images were there, they yielded to the protestations of Melanie, *The Echo's* lab tech, and shuffled back to the office to wait for the sheets to go through the dryer.

"Must be something pretty sexy in these," Melanie quipped, dropping eleven 8/10 glossy prints onto Sarah's desk. "Amazing what some people get off on nowadays."

The photos showed the evidence. "Bullet proof!" Sarah and Ernie exclaimed in chorus. There on the prints were the signatures of the persons responsible for the commitment of Timothy Kenneth Caulfield, age 19, for treatment at the Rose Hills Institute. There was the diagnosis: *bipolar disorder, dementia, paranoia.* There were the symptoms: *hearing voices, obsessive fear, self-destructive behavior, etc.,* and then the treatment prescribed: *frontal lobotomy brain surgery.* The signatures on the authorization were *J. Kenneth Caulfield, father,* and *Vernon Milosovic, M.D., attending physician* (and surely then no longer a licensed one)!

* * * *

By Monday noon, Rose Hills Institute's Creighton Bingham was troubled. He had received no word from Sarah Baker on Saturday, and an evening call to the Sheraton had only produced the information that the party had checked out. There was no word this morning. Dr. McKenzie had reserved time for an interview, and was impatiently calling to know where "this damned Baker woman" was.

Bingham telephoned the office of *Mind and Body* magazine in Monterey and heard a recording: "You have reached the editorial office of *Mind and Body*. We are unable to speak with you at the moment, but please leave your name and number and your call will be returned. Watch for our inaugural issue November 13. It's certain to be a collectors item." *Beep* . . .

* * * *

Three days later the editorial seemed to be writing itself, and with every sentence Sarah put on paper, typing almost in a trance on her father's old Underwood, she felt euphoria. She so enjoyed the sensation that she didn't know when she'd crossed the line. Ernie knew.

He had written the lead story for the week's issue,

with the exposé of Ursula Ketterman's murder, professionally articulated, civilly stated, thoroughly documented, and destined to be a media bombshell. He had not disclosed the name or whereabouts of Rose Hills Institute. Now he was carefully composing a letter to the careful Mr. Bingham at Rose Hills who, in his opinion, was a worthy and professional gentleman, deserving a great deal more than an unreturned phone call from a non-existent magazine. At his desk in the corner by the window Ernie sat back, left elbow on the arm of his chair, chin in his hand, watching the love of his life.

The sun had gone down and there was no one left in the building except the two of them. Everything else for tomorrow's edition had been finalized by mid afternoon. They would print the facts they had learned of the murder of Ursula Ketterman, the perfidy of Kenneth Caulfield, and the tragedy of Timothy, knowing that *The Echo* might then cease to exist. At least the story will get published, they had reasoned. Their money was gone, and whether or not there would be an *Echo* next week somehow seemed suborinate to the fact that they had done what they set out to do. They'd just have to see what the financial and legal fallout would be. It was a lead pipe cinch the story would generate wire service coverage.

* * * *

For the past 45 minutes Sarah had been completely immersed in her copy, still beating on Caulfield's decomposing coffin, oblivious to the fact that Ernie was even in the room. She had to write this editorial, he knew. But did she have any idea of what the process was doing to her, the aura of ugliness it could overlay onto a radiant, beautiful face?

The scenario seemed patently obvious to Sarah: Timothy had been motivated by the desperate need to appear strong, macho, virile before his friends. After the murder he was frantic, guilt ridden, too emotionally weak to hide the torment he felt inside. Then the flagpole episode, and what might he do next? That, she reasoned, was the conundrum facing his father. Kenneth Caulfield had built a dynasty and was rich and famous, even if he'd achieved it by screwing people like her father. If others had a kinder view of him, so what? Her image was true to the treatment her father had experienced, and the suffering it had caused her mother.

Caulfield had put everything in his life on a balance. On the left was success; on the right was his son. On the left he could ride in parades, have the power of a Publisher, the respect of a Patriarch, be called Senator. On the right there was a troubled boy, scandal and disgrace as a father and citizen. And he'd made his choice: the Rose Garden Institute took care of it for him with a knife. Now for his beloved Timothy there was no more guilt, no more flagpoles, and just incidentally no more chance of making some jackass remark about what really happened that afternoon in the greenhouse.

And wasn't it fortunate, Mr. C., that the noble

Caulfield name remained unsullied? The more Sarah thought about it, the more righteous she felt. And didn't Sheriff Russell suddenly have money to buy himself a ranch in the highlands just in time to provide a place to tuck away out of sight the body without a mind, the boy who was once your son?

Sarah was barely typing now, but she could see her thoughts as clearly as if they were projected on a screen. Okay, some of our evidence was illegally obtained, and some of it's circumstantial. Hey, this is the Free Press of America, Mr. C., you've heard about that! In print you can be tried, convicted and hung by the neck before lunch. Do I hate the rest of your family? Not at all. But how I hate the ground you were buried under! And those kids in the greenhouse, those goddam rotten kids—"

Sarah was talking aloud, unknowing, her face contorted with the zeal of condemnation.

Ernie walked across the room, knelt beside her, and quietly put his arms around her. Suddenly aware, she took a deep breath, then leaned back in her chair.

"I guess I kind'a got into this, Ernie."

"I guess you did. Let me bring you some coffee. I need to tell you something."

* * * *

The coffee wasn't fresh, but served its purpose. They drank it with creamer and enough sugar to get it down.

When their cups were empty, and nothing but banalities had been spoken, Sarah looked quizzically at Ernie.

"Let's walk a bit," he said.

It was dark but not completely. To the west, the sky still held the faint palette of a dramatic sunset, thanks to an offshore wind that had blown dust from the farms and pollution from the coastal cities out to sea. Another Santa Ana. To the east, the moon was just over the ridge, almost full. He held her arm lightly as they walked along the road.

"I want to tell you why I came to work for your father. I'd had two people selling me on this guy. You did it personally when you wrote about him at Berkeley, Professor Jewison did it professionally. What came through from you both was his character. Okay, that was reason enough. Besides, it was supposed the be the career move I needed. But I knew inside myself the strongest pull that brought me here was you. When you came home to take on the paper, I was in Disneyland. Then you married Martin and my roller coaster crashed. I'd found you, then I'd lost you. But now I've found you again."

"Am I a keeper?"

"My dear, dear Sarah, you know the answer to that." They turned back to the office. Ernie put his chair beside her desk. "Here's what I've been trying to say, Sarah. and it would be a lot easier if I could write it, but that wouldn't work."

"What wouldn't work?"

"I've been digging into this investigation not to muck-rake, but to honor your father, and to prove to you how much I love you. I know this story has become the most important thing in your life. But we've got all we need now, Sarah, haven't we? Isn't this enough?"

He waited. She didn't answer.

Then he asked quietly, "Is anything ever enough?" At this she flared.

"What on earth do you mean by a question like that? This isn't about muckraking. This is about truth! The truth has got to be told, Ernie, the whole truth, every-thing. We're almost there. And even if we can't touch Russell, we're going to find that other kid somehow. The whole truth, Ernie, the whole—goddam truth!"

Ernie looked at her quietly. "Can you take the whole truth, Sarah?"

"Of course I can. Whatever it is! What do you mean?"

"Sarah—that other kid was your brother."

Time stopped. Seconds ceased to tick. Until Sarah locked her eyes into Ernie's, and saw in the pain there that he had spoken honestly. Georgie!

Shattered, she screamed in silence, crumbling inside. Everything went into slow motion, without sound. Then she rallied herself and ran out the door. And ran. Until she could stand to run no more, to the century-old church where her mother and father were buried. By their head-stones she sat sobbing, exhausted and devastated.

Quiet came at last. Sarah's burning obsession with Caulfield had unearthed a smoldering secret in her own family. Memories flooded over her in waves, fighting with her questions. She saw the lifeless girl in the greenhouse, a frantic mother, Timothy in terror, the "other kid," - her brother - shielding Timmy yet again, just as he had done for years. She saw Georgie in high school, lifted on the shoulders of his teammates, cheered for making the winning touchdown against Paso Robles. She loved him. and his dear, dear family. I'm their Aunt Sarah. And then—Caulfield's other children. For the first time, probably for the first time ever, she thought of the lives of Caulfield's other children.

The darkened church behind her stretched its steeple up to heaven. In the stillness there was music, a hymn her mother loved to sing, She sat there on the grass and thought about the words . . .

When Sarah returned to the office it was 2:00 a.m. The door was unlocked. She sat at her desk, her father's desk, and looked at the two photographs there; a picture of her parents with her brother and herself, taken during their early days in Oak Hills, and a picture of Georgie and his family. She was in it. Everyone was smiling. She turned it over, and saw a dog-eared card stuck into the back of the frame. In George Baker's unmistakable hand was written: "In my Father's house . . ."

Sarah sat silently. Minutes passed. Then quietly she whispered, "Yes."

Her thoughts turned to Ernie. He was willing to give up his career for love of her. She climbed the creaky stairway and found him lying across his bed asleep, still dressed. For a few minutes she looked around the room. She could feel her father here, her childhood, her womanhood, her life. Carefully she took off Ernie's shoes, then covered him and lay down next to him. He stirred, and realized she was there. He started to say something. Sarah put her fingers to his lips and shushed him.

"We have enough now, Ernie. Enough." She put her arm across him.

Two hours later they woke and looked at the clock. Ernie stretched and yawned. "Well, I have a deadline to meet or I just might lose my job."

"What job, you unemployed and unemployable stud? Yes, Mr. Hemmingway, it's way past deadline, but I'm the publisher." She looked at his face, stroked the stubble on his chin. "Thank you, Ernie," she said.

They walked down the steps to the office and Sarah wrote a new editorial. The last two paragraphs read:

"This investigative story represents an editorial departure for *The Echo*, but it has been in preparation for months, and even years. George Baker, our founding publisher, began the investigation in 1954, when events described here re-galvanized his commitment to report the whole truth about issues the public needed to know. Most of the facts of the case, hidden ever since the tragic death of Ursula Ketterman in 1942, have been uncovered by the diligence of Ernest Marshall Hemmingway, who discussed the investigation many times with his publisher. George Baker did not live to see the truth discovered or the story printed, yet this story is his, a tribute to his integrity.

"It is with utmost sorrow that we write the whole truth here. Sorrow for the pain it inflicts. The greatest sorrow, an eternal one, is for the loss of the life of Ursula Ketterman, and the desolation and torment of her mother and all of her family. And also the family of Timothy Caulfield. For those touched in any way by this unspeakable pain, we beseech the mercies of Heaven."

Sarah put the copy in a folder and placed it carefully in the center of her desk. It was 5:45, beginning to show the dawn. They'd been waiting for this Friday. She touched the corner of the blotter lightly, glanced at Ernie, silhouetted at the door, then stepped outside and clicked the lock. She turned back to face the window. Beneath the name of *The Echo* was written, "The Whole Truth." She dropped the key into Ernie's pocket and slid her arm through his.

Afterword

Although it was originally published as fiction, E. M. Hemmingway's 1969 novel, *Yellow Ink* (446 pp, R. J. Carruthers and Company, Toronto), has been assigned reading in journalism schools for more than a decade.

Hemmingway was nearing completion of the manuscript during the tragic days of the South East Asian conflict, when publishing contracts were at a premium. He arranged with his local newspaper to put the first 50 pages of the book onto newsprint, in the format of a penny shopper, and sent copies in plain brown envelopes to the legal departments and editors of publishing houses across North America.

The mailing created a firestorm of interest. Hemmingway dedicated the book to his writing teacher, Arthur McKinney, "who did something with his life."

FCM Montego Bay 1986

Footnote to history

In 1949, Portuguese neuropsychiatrist Antonio Egas Moniz was awarded the Nobel Prize for inventing the procedure of the prefrontal lobotomy. He had first observed in an experiment at Yale University that severing the frontal lobes of the brain of a disturbed primate had seemed to produce a calming effect.

Between 1939 and 1951, more than 18,000 lobotomies were performed in the United States alone. The procedure was sometimes abused as a method of controlling undesirable behavior, instead of as a last-resort therapeutic procedure for desperately ill patients. An early example of this, widely covered in the media, was Rosemary Kennedy, whose father allegedly insisted the procedure be applied to treat her relatively mild retardation, a condition reportedly caused at birth by delaying her delivery to wait for a male doctor. Lobotomies were abandoned as a treatment when therapeutic drugs were developed in the 1950s.

Finally

Endless gratitude to Robert J. Fleming, friend, mentor and role model in helping amateurs and experts realize potential and talents often hidden. To him I owe my career in photography, writing, and publishing.

With our longtime teammate Stewart Lancaster, Bob Fleming launched PACE magazine in 1964, a thrilling laboratory of journalism ahead of its time.

and

Sincerest thanks to you, dear reader,
for waiting this long for Friday.

Made in the USA
Columbia, SC
28 May 2019